KU-437-937

The Trail of Vengeance

Arthur Henry Gooden

CENTER POINT LARGE PRINT
THORNDIKE, MAINE

This Center Point Large Print edition is published
in the year 2016 by arrangement with
Golden West Literary Agency.

Copyright © 1939 by Arthur Henry Gooden.
Copyright © renewed 1967 by the Estate of
Arthur Henry Gooden.

All rights reserved.

First US edition: Phoenix Books.

The text of this Large Print edition is unabridged.
In other aspects, this book may vary
from the original edition.

Set in 16-point Times New Roman type.

ISBN: 978-1-68324-012-9 (hardcover)
ISBN: 978-1-68324-016-7 (paperback)

Library of Congress Cataloging-in-Publication Data

Names: Gooden, Arthur Henry, 1879–1971, author.
Title: The trail of vengeance / Arthur Henry Gooden.
Description: Center Point Large Print edition. | Thorndike, Maine :
Center Point Large Print, 2016. | ©1939
Identifiers: LCCN 2016011396| ISBN 9781683240129 (hardcover :
alk. paper) | ISBN 9781683240167 (pbk. : alk. paper)
Subjects: LCSH: Large type books. | GSAFD: Western stories.
Classification: LCC PS3513.O4767 T73 2016 | DDC 813/.52—dc23
LC record available at http://lccn.loc.gov/2016011396

Printed and bound in Great Britain
by TJ International Ltd, Padstow, Cornwall

The Trail of Vengeance

Contents

Chapter One

Mystery at Mexican Wells

Breck kept the gray horse moving steadily—an easy running-walk. Shimmering heat-waves tortured his eyes, and vagrant puffs of hot wind sent little dust-devils dancing across the sand dunes.

The single canteen had long since been emptied. Breck had expected to find water at Coyote Springs. The long dry season had left only a sunbaked mudhole. He was reasonably certain there would be water at Mexican Wells, some three hours further on the way.

Far to the left lifted the grim escarpment of the Panamints, bulking vaguely against the shimmering golden glare of the hot horizon, and sprawling a serpentine course from the Cactus Mountains was the wide wash of the Arroyo Seco.

It was in the dry sands of the Arroyo Seco that the cool waters of Mexican Wells eternally bubbled up from subterranean depths.

There was a dust haze down there. Breck reined the tired horse and stared with speculative eyes. Dust might mean horsemen—and horsemen might mean danger.

His own home land, this vast place of bristling cacti and greasewood and sand dunes, with the hills lifting beyond, where lay the rich rolling pastures of the Calico. His own country—yet because of men who sought his life—also an enemy country.

He swung from saddle and scrambled up the steep ascent of a lone butte, pausing now and again to wipe sweaty face and drawlingly reproach the unfriendly sun and the desert in general.

A final effort brought him panting to the top, where he sought the shade of an overhanging ledge and reached for his binoculars.

Horsemen, as he suspected. They stood out distinct under the powerful glass. Three riders, and armed. Sunlight flashed from rifle barrels.

They were headed for a narrow gap in the low rugged hills rising sheer from the desert floor some two miles below Mexican Wells.

Breck knew the place. Painted Canyon was little more than a narrow gorge, walled by high cliffs colored by the violent hues of the desert.

He continued to watch until suddenly the dark narrow mouth of the canyon hid them from view, then thoughtfully he made his way down to his horse.

What he had seen vaguely disturbed Breck. He could not think of any legitimate purpose the men would have in Painted Canyon. They might possibly be Circle B riders, but hardly probable. Cattle were not likely to stray into this arid region during the hot, dry summer months.

Breck shrugged the troublesome thoughts aside. The important matter now was to make Mexican Wells. There was nothing to do but keep on his way and at the same time avoid an encounter with the unknown horsemen. He could not risk being seen until he knew the identity of the mysterious strangers.

He rode on, alert gray eyes wary.

A green fringe of trees marked the little stream made by the overflow from the springs. It was not much more than a trickle that soon vanished to the subterranean channel beneath the sands of the big wash.

The gray needed no urging. The smell of water was in his nostrils. Head high, ears twitching, the horse plunged down the trail that wound between great boulders and clutching cactus.

The camp had a deserted air. Breck was not surprised. Mexican Wells was used only during the semi-annual roundups of the spring and fall. Circle B riders seldom ventured so far from the home ranch during the hot months.

Breck drew rein, suddenly disturbed and fighting the maddened Silver King's impatience to reach the little stream that flowed from the springs in an enclosure between the pole corral and the cabin half hidden under huge cottonwood trees.

Instinct warned him that there was something wrong with the picture.

Suddenly he knew what was wrong. With something like a shock he stared at the wisp of pale blue smoke lifting lazily above the roof of the old camp cabin under the cottonwood trees.

A woman appeared in the doorway. She was quite short and plump and wore a white dress and a blue print kitchen apron. A wisp of loosened white hair fell over one ear and a pair of steel-rimmed spectacles was perched on her nose. All in all, there was a pleasantly wholesome and grandmotherly look about the old lady that was not in keeping with the shotgun pressed to her shoulder.

"What do you want, young man?" Her tone was crisp and businesslike. "You better put up your hands while we talk," she added. "Elevate *pronto*, as you cowfolk say out in this wild west land."

Breck grinned, struggled to keep Silver King from bolting to the creek.

"This horse is mad for water, ma'am," he pointed out. "I can't hold him if I put up my hands."

"You do what I say!" commanded the old lady severely.

"We sure crave water, ma'am," argued Breck. "Found Coyote Springs a dry mudhole. The desert's no place to be caught without water handy."

She eyed him doubtfully over the barrel of the gun.

"You do look bad, the pair of you," she admitted worriedly. She shook her head. "It isn't for me to refuse a drink of water to man nor beast. Wouldn't be Christian." She lowered the gun a trifle. "Go and get your drink, young man, but mind you—no tricks—or I'll shoot—"

Breck gave Silver King his head and with a rush they were at the creek. Breck slid from saddle, stiffened as he heard the old lady's crisp voice behind him.

"Don't move! Stand as you are—your back toward me—and put up your hands—"

He obeyed. There was a note in her voice that warned him this astonishing old lady was not to be trifled with.

She came up close, plucked his long six-gun from holster, then deftly removed the rifle from saddle-boot.

"Now you can have your drink," she said in a relieved tone.

Breck's grin was sheepish. It was an experience unique in his life to have an old woman hold him up and take his guns away.

"*Gracias, Señora*," he thanked her politely.

"I can't say you are welcome," retorted the old lady tartly. "But bad and mean as the lot of you are, it isn't for *me* to see you die for want of a drink of water."

Shotgun in hands, the confiscated weapons at her feet, she watched with alert eyes while Breck filled the canteen and drank. He sighed gratefully, refilled the canteen and returned it to the saddle.

"Good water," he said, smiling at her. "Cold as ice."

The old lady nodded. "Funny about that water," she observed. "The way it bubbles up out of this dry old creek bed. A queer place, this desert. Never did understand how the springs got such an outlandish name as Mexican Wells."

"It happened a long time ago," Breck told her. "A Mexican was lost out here—" He waved toward the brown Cactus Mountains—"they found him lying less than ten yards from the springs—dead. He couldn't quite make it—reach the water that would have saved his life. Water is a precious thing out here in the desert," he added.

"Makes a good story," said the old lady, nodding her head. "Well, young man, now you and your horse have had your drink of water, you can ride back to where you came from."

Breck eyed his guns. She shook her head.

"I'll keep them for you," she said briskly. "It will teach you a lesson—riding in so smart and trying to frighten us away from this place."

Breck eyed her with growing wonder.

"We're sick and tired of you cowboys coming round with your threats," she went on placidly.

"Jane and I are not to be frightened. We've made up our minds to homestead this place."

"I reckon what you say is the truth, ma'am," Breck said, looking at her respectfully. "I reckon you shore don't scare easily." He glanced ruefully at six-gun and rifle lying at her feet.

"It's real cowardly of you—trying to terrorize two lone women," she pointed out.

"Who do you think I am, ma'am?" Breck's tone was curious.

"You needn't pretend, young man!" She gave him an indignant look.

"I'm not pretending, ma'am," he protested. "I've just come all the way from the Texas Panhandle. I have a cattle ranch down there."

There was frank disbelief in her eyes.

"You mean you can stand there and tell me you are not from the Circle B?"

"I'm riding that way," Breck admitted cautiously. He eyed her worriedly. "What's the Circle B got to do with your troubles?"

"The Circle B has everything to do with our troubles," declared the old lady. "Time and again Circle B riders have been here—warning us to get out." There was a suspicious tremble in the placid voice. "Why, I do believe they have threatened Jane with dreadful things—if we don't leave by the end of the week." She shook her head worriedly. "I do declare if the week isn't already up," she murmured half to herself.

"That's why those men were here to see her this morning."

Breck looked at her with frowning eyes. He was finding it difficult to visualize his old father, or grizzled Jim Hawker, veteran foreman of the Circle B, threatening to do violence on two lone females—even if they *were* nesters on Circle B range.

He squatted on his heels, cowboy fashion and fished tobacco and cigarette papers from a shirt pocket. The old lady's eyes sparkled angrily from behind her steel-rimmed spectacles.

"I thought I told you to get on your horse and get away from this place," she reminded.

"I want to talk to you," smiled Breck. He deftly made a cigarette and as deftly flicked match against his thumbnail. The old lady watched the performance with fascinated eyes.

Breck drew thoughtfully on his cigarette.

"Who is Jane?" he wanted to know.

"Why—Jane is my niece," she stammered, taken off her guard by the abruptness of the question. The pink in her face deepened. "Now see here, young man—don't you think I'm going to answer *your* questions!"

"It will do you no harm to answer a few questions," Breck said quietly. "In fact—quite the opposite."

She seemed impressed.

"Well, ask on," she said finally, and sighed.

"No use for you to hold that heavy shotgun on me," suggested Breck. "You're getting tired—and anyway—you have *my* guns."

"Maybe you're right," agreed Jane's aunt with another sigh. "It weighs a ton by now. I think I'll sit down on this stump while you talk." She sat down and placed the shotgun at her feet. "You seem like a nice young man," she added. "Not like those cruel-faced cowboys who've been pestering us."

"*Gracias, Señora.*" Breck chuckled, then his tone became grave. "Your niece is not home, I gather, Mrs.—"

Her eyes twinkled good-humoredly.

"I'm Jane's Aunt Sally—if that's what you're wanting to know." Her tone was suddenly worried. "No, Jane is not home. She went off some place this morning. Those men were trying to find out where she went."

Breck nodded thoughtfully. He seemed to be drawing lines in the sand with a piece of stick he had picked up.

"Do you know anything about brands?" he queried suddenly.

Aunt Sally nodded brightly. "You mean those marks they put on cows and horses?"

"Perhaps you happened to notice the marks on the horses these men had this morning," Breck went on.

"Oh, yes, I did. One of the men rode right up to

the door. He was on a nice black horse and I noticed the brand."

"Was the brand like this?" Breck indicated the picture he had drawn in the sand.

Aunt Sally got up from the stump. Evidently she had lost her fear of this tall, quiet-voiced young stranger with the steady gray eyes. Disregarding the shotgun, she went to Breck's side and peered curiously.

"Oh, no, indeed!" she exclaimed. "The brand on the black horse was like a horseshoe with a little 's' in the middle."

Breck nodded grimly.

"Have you ever seen this sort of mark on any of the horses ridden by the cowboys who've been threatening you and your niece?" Again he indicated the scrawl in the sand.

Aunt Sally shook her head. "No," she averred in a bewildered tone. "They have always been like the horseshoe mark I told you about."

"This picture I've drawn here in the dirt is the brand of the Circle B," Breck told her quietly.

Aunt Sally's bewilderment grew.

"I—I don't understand," she confessed. "What do you mean?"

"I mean I've proved that the men who have been trying to run you away from Mexican Wells are not Circle B riders." There was a chill look in Breck's eyes. "I think I know where those men came from—and who sent them." He sprang to his feet and the old lady drew back, startled by his fierce expression.

"Who—who are *you?*" she quavered.

"I'm Breck Allen, son of the man who owns the Circle B Ranch."

Amazement was in the look Aunt Sally gave him.

"You are sure it is not your father who has been trying to terrorize us?"

"I'm positive!" declared Breck.

Aunt Sally beamed at him. "That's good news, young man. I took a liking to you right from the first."

"I'm glad you didn't pull the trigger of that gun," he chuckled.

"It's not loaded," placidly confessed Aunt Sally. "I'm scared to death of guns."

He gave her an awed look. "My God!" he muttered. "Don't you ever try to run that sort of bluff again."

"It worked," she reminded, with a twinkling look at the confiscated guns. And then, as if sensing his thoughts, Aunt Sally paled. "Maybe I was an old fool," she finished. "You could have killed me—if you'd wanted to—if you'd been like those men—" She shuddered.

Breck retrieved his guns and regarded her with oddly troubled eyes.

"Have you any idea where your niece went riding?" he wanted to know.

"It was some place she called the Painted Canyon," Aunt Sally told him. "Why?"—reading the quick dismay in his face—"I didn't let on to those men where she was—"

Breck was flinging his lean length into the saddle. He smiled down at her encouragingly.

"I'll be riding out that way. Don't worry."

The great silver-gray stallion reared, pawed the air and fled up the trail, leaving behind a suddenly very frightened old woman who watched until horse and rider were lost from view in the chaparral.

Chapter Two

The Painted Canyon

Breck was frankly alarmed regarding the intentions of the three strangers he had seen riding into Painted Canyon. His encounter with Aunt Sally had disclosed their identity. They were the same men who had ridden into Mexican Wells that morning, looking for the old lady's niece.

There was fear in Breck's eyes as he sent the gray horse at reckless speed through the chaparral, fear for the girl, up there in that lonely canyon. And there was bitter anger in him against Val Stamper of the Horseshoe. The latter's motive in sending his riders to pose as Circle B men in an attempt to drive the girl and her aunt from Mexican Wells was a baffling mystery that must wait for later investigation. Val Stamper was not one to show his hand. His ways were dark and devious. The man was up to some devil's mischief. There was more than met the eye in his infamous attack upon two lone women. Val Stamper was playing for bigger stakes than Mexican Wells.

The maze of prickly pear and vicious *cholla* gave way to a boulder-strewn slope. It was a bleak and desolate scene. Breck found himself wondering what strange lure could have induced a young girl to venture alone into the wilds of Painted Canyon. He had a shrewd suspicion that the answer to the conundrum would explain why she wanted to possess Mexican Wells—perhaps explain Val Stamper's sinister activities.

The rust-red cliffs that marked the canyon's narrow entrance loomed directly ahead.

Breck slowed his horse to a walk.

That crevice-like portal was the only possible way of entering the gorge—and the only exit—for a horseman.

One could ride up the canyon for some four or five miles between sheer, towering cliffs to a tumbled mass of volcanic slabs impassable to a horse. To penetrate deeper into the maze of canyons beyond, one must proceed on foot.

Breck was certain that the girl and the men trailing her were still somewhere up the gorge. Jane may have discovered her danger in time to find cover for herself and horse. He fervently hoped this would be the case. Otherwise he feared the worst. Aunt Sally had intimated that violence had been threatened if the ultimatum to abandon Mexican Wells was disregarded.

He drew rein, eyes and ears alert.

The stillness of the place oppressed him. It was an ominous quiet that filled him with foreboding. Overhead a buzzard soared against the blue.

The silence was shattered by the reverberating

crash of a rifle. Loud, profane shouts echoed from the canyon, and Breck now heard the sudden staccato beat of hoofs.

A rider, on a pinto horse, spurred furiously into the open from the painted cliffs. The rifle roared again. The pinto went down, lay shuddering.

Breck spurred alongside and reached out a hand to the slim young girl struggling free from the dying horse. He had a momentary glimpse of a pale oval of face under wind-blown dark hair, a quick, questioning look from wide-open dark eyes, and she was up behind him.

The gray horse fled down the slope with his double burden.

Breck was acutely aware of the girl's clinging arms—of her quickened breath against his neck.

He knew a fight could not be avoided. With the girl at his back he dare not risk making a running fight of it. Silver King could not outrun a bullet.

He heard the girl's voice in his ear.

"They're coming," she said. "They are out of the canyon—"

There was no hint of panic in the low tones. Breck knew by the caress of her wind-blown hair against his neck that she was again looking back at their pursuers. She spoke again.

"One of them has jumped from his horse . . . He's going to shoot—"

"A top-hand girl—this Jane," was Breck's

thought as he swung the gray behind a boulder. "Smart as the crack of a whip!"

They heard the screaming whine of a bullet, followed by the crash of the rifle.

Breck grinned round into the dark eyes at his shoulder.

"Thanks for the tip. That *hombre* was shooting close."

The dark eyes, so near to his own, regarded him gravely, searchingly, then suddenly they returned his smile.

"Now what?" She spoke coolly. "Where do we go from here—mister?"

The drumming of horses' hoofs drew down the stony slope. Breck eyed their surroundings. It was an ideal place for a defensive battle.

"We'll fight it out here," he told the girl grimly.

She slid from the horse and Breck leaped from saddle. He wanted to stop those riders before they could reach the opening between the tumbled masses of granite.

"They've pulled into the brush," exclaimed the girl. She was peering through an opening between the boulders.

Breck drew his rifle from saddle-boot and crouched by her side. The men had sought cover, obviously disconcerted by the changed conditions. Breck's sudden appearance on the scene would puzzle them.

He looked round at his companion.

"They can't figure me out," he chuckled. "I've got 'em guessing."

"They're a cowardly lot!" declared the girl fiercely. "I've killed rattlesnakes—and those men are worse than rattlesnakes!" Her small brown hand tightened over the butt of a gun in the holster buckled to her slim waist.

She was about twenty-two or -three, Breck decided. Her eyes were a deep blue, the sort of midnight blue that seems black under stress of excitement. She wore overalls, pulled over high-heeled boots, and a man's blue flannel shirt, open at the throat. A loosely-knotted bandana, the color of maize, gave a touch of brightness to her dusty, masculine attire. Undeniably lovely, with her warm dark brown hair and short, straight nose. Breck liked the self-reliant tilt of the well-molded chin. No clinging vine, this Jane person, yet attractively feminine enough to quicken the heart of any man.

She was eyeing him curiously.

"I can't figure you out, either," she went on. "How did you happen to be johnny-on-the-spot?"

"We'll talk about it later," promised Breck. "Right now, I think our friends are hatching up some scheme to finish this business."

A voice hailed them from the chaparral.

"Hi! *hombre*! What's yore game—hornin' in on our play?"

"Come over here and find out," jeered Breck.

A chorus of oaths answered him, and again—silence.

"They seem slightly upset," chuckled Breck. He looked at the girl. There was a weary droop to the slight, boyish figure. "Sit down," he told her gently. "It's been a tough day for you!"

She obeyed, threw a longing glance at the canteen on the saddle.

"It's been hell—up there in that dreadful canyon—hiding from those beasts." She forced a wan smile. "I could do with a drink of water, mister. A long, long drink—"

He waved at the canteen. "Help yourself." His alert gaze was again on the slope above. "It's good water . . . Your aunt said so—"

"My *aunt!*" Jane's astonished stare fastened on the tall young man crouched at the crevice between the boulders. "When—when did you meet Aunt Sally?"

Another shout from the brush-clad slope interrupted her.

"Hi! *hombre!* We want that gal down there an' we shore aim to git her."

"Go to hell!" Breck called back cheerfully. "All you *hombres* will get is hot lead!"

He grinned round at the girl. She was eyeing him with frowning intentness, a hand on the canteen.

"Who are you?" she wanted to know.

He gestured impatiently. "Get your drink—and

26

if you can handle that gun you wear—don't be afraid to use it. There's trouble coming—"

She obeyed, took a long pull at the canteen and replaced it on the saddle.

"I'll tell you this much," Breck said, as Jane resumed her place by his side, "I'm your friend. It was your aunt who told me you were up in Painted Canyon—"

The whine of a bullet interrupted him—the crash of a rifle.

"They'll try to get below us," Breck told the girl. "You keep a watch on that ridge, yonder. Tell me if you see anything stirring. I'll take care of this side."

She nodded, held her gun ready.

"I'll do the shooting," Breck said. "Too far for your .32. Just tell me if you see anything moving on the ridge."

The spokesman hailed them again.

"That gal's a nester, feller. We want her!"

"Who are you?" called Breck. "What's your outfit?"

"Circle B," came the answer.

"You're a liar!" retorted Breck. "I'm Circle B— and the Circle B doesn't make war on lone women."

There was a little gasp from the girl by his side. He said curtly, without glancing at her:

"You watch that ridge. They want to pull off a quick play while they keep me talking—"

"Who the hell are you, mister?" called the voice from the brush.

"Breck Allen—of the Circle B—"

Jane sprang to her feet with a startled exclamation.

"*You*—then you *are* a Circle B man—the owner—"

"The owner's son," Breck told her briefly. "Watch that ridge," he repeated. "It's good night if they get below us."

She hesitated, looked down at him doubtfully, studied the keen brown face pressed close to the crevice. He flashed her an impatient glance.

"Watch that ridge!" he repeated harshly. "Never mind wondering about *me!*"

"But—but those men up there—are Circle B men!" She gestured. "Those devils up there are from the Circle B!"

She stood irresolute, gun clenched in hand, yet her gaze again fastened on the ridge. They could hear the men loudly discussing Breck. Laughs and jeers floated down the hill.

"Reckon that'll be news for the sheriff—to hear Breck Allen's back on the range," shouted a voice.

"We'll save the sheriff a job o' work," chortled another voice. "So young Breck Allen's back in town! If that don't beat hell!"

Jane said softly, "I think something is moving —up on the ridge . . . it's a man—behind that clump of barrel cactus—"

28

"*Gracias*," muttered Breck. His rifle crashed. A howl of pain and rage answered the shot; a man jerked into view, half ran, half tumbled behind a sheltering boulder.

"Good shot, mister," the girl said coolly.

"Hurt bad, Cisco?" called a voice.

"Hurt plenty," grumbled the man behind the boulder. "Took a piece clean outer my ear."

His fellow desperadoes jeered.

"Yore ears always was too big, Cisco. Mebbe he'll trim the other one for yuh."

Cisco cursed them.

"They're tough *hombres*," Breck told the girl.

She nodded. "Killers," she said. "I heard them talking—up in Painted Canyon—when I was hiding. They were planning to kill me in cold blood." She repressed a shudder. "It was dreadful to hear them!"

There was pity in the quick look he gave her.

"You poor kid."

His attention returned to the brush-clad slope. Cisco's two companions were talking the situation over. Their hoarse voices reached down the hill faintly.

"Perhaps they'll give up—go away," hoped Jane.

"They're tough *hombres*," repeated Breck. "Their kind don't give up easily."

A voice hailed them from the chaparral.

"You ain't gotta chance to git away from us,

29

Allen. You come outer there with yore hands reachin' for the sky an' we won't harm yuh. We'll let the sheriff 'tend to *you,* Allen. All we want is the gal."

"Come down here and talk it over," invited Breck.

The spokesman cursed him fluently.

"We kin wait here longer than you stick it out!" he shouted. "We got plenty food an' water. We'll set here till you come out like I said."

There was silence, broken only by muttered oaths from the wounded man behind the boulder.

"It seems like a stalemate," Jane said, and then curiously, "They seem to know you rather well—and yet you claim they are not from the Circle B—"

"The Circle B doesn't hire their sort," Breck assured her grimly. "At least—not in my time."

She frowned at this. "Then you don't really know they are *not* Circle B men," she said pointedly. "I gather you have been away from the ranch . . . that you are on the dodge from the sheriff—"

"You're getting warm," grinned Breck. "Been down in the Texas Panhandle the last seven years —but I'm not exactly dodging the sheriff."

"But you don't really know about these men," persisted Jane. "I've been warned several times by Circle B men to leave Mexican Wells—"

"It's a trick," muttered Breck. He looked round

at her. Jane was startled by the cold fury in the gray eyes. "I have already proved to your aunt that these men—and the others who have been threatening you—are Horseshoe men—"

The girl's eyes widened. "But the Horseshoe Ranch belongs to Mr. Stamper," she demurred. "Mr. Stamper has been very kind to me. I've met him at his bank in Calico. You are crazy—to accuse *him!*"

Breck was staring intently up the slope. There was a tight look about his mouth. The doubt in Jane's eyes grew as she studied him.

"It is all very puzzling—and terrible," she said in a low voice. "I'd like to believe you, but to accuse Mr. Stamper is very upsetting. I can't believe for a moment that he is back of all this horrible affair. Why—I've met his daughter, Della. Such an attractive girl. She invited Aunt Sally and me to visit her at their home in town."

Breck's look reached round to her again. The chill light had left his eyes and there was a hint of amusement in his slow smile.

"Della must have changed a lot since I saw her last." He chuckled. "She was all legs and red hair and impudence. But that was seven years ago. Della was only a kid of thirteen or so."

"She's lovely now," murmured Jane. She was watching the ridge sharply. "I—I think that man is trying it again," she added in a matter-of-fact tone.

"*Gracias*," muttered Breck. "No fooling this time," he added grimly.

It was Cisco's last attempt to make the ridge. Nor was there an outcry from him as Breck's rifle roared. Jane saw the desperado stagger from behind a clump of greasewood and collapse to a shuddering heap. Her face paled.

"You—you killed him," she said in a low tone, not looking at Breck.

He shrugged his shoulders, lowered the smoking rifle and ejected the empty shell.

A brief silence followed the sudden passing of Cisco. Breck's deadly efficiency with his rifle was worrying the remaining pair up in the chaparral.

"Damn yuh, Allen!" The spokesman's voice was convulsed with fury—and dismay. "We'll git yuh for that—for killin' Cisco!"

Breck flung a shot into the brush. An answering fusillade poured back. For a few moments the air was filled with the vicious whine of leaden hail.

It was a futile effort on the part of the desperadoes, as they must have known.

"We're safe as long as we can keep them from getting below us," Breck reassured the girl. He looked at her unsmilingly. "Do you still think those men out there are from the Circle B?" Something like bitterness edged his quiet voice.

Jane flushed. "No!" she exclaimed. "No! I've

been stupid!" Her low voice trembled. "You—you must be hating me!"

The hard light passed from Breck's eyes as he continued to look at her.

"I'm not blaming you," he said honestly. "They've been riding you hard. It's a nasty mess." He smiled. "Aunt Sally and I are already good friends. I hope I can be your friend, too—"

Relief showed in her lively, expressive face, an answering friendly smile quirked the corners of a generous and lovely mouth.

"Aunt Sally is a good picker," she told him with a hint of demureness. "I can't do better than follow her lead." She shivered, glanced up the slope. "I think you already have proved a friend in need—a good friend—"

The desperado's voice came again from the hillside.

"Listen, feller!" The man's tone was worried. "Reckon we'll call it a day an' be on our way from here."

"I'm not keeping you," retorted Breck.

"We aim to git our broncs an' hightail it *pronto* —only we don't want yore hot lead flyin' our way."

"Come out where I can see you—with your hands up," was Breck's response. "Both of you!"

There was a silence as the two men argued between themselves. Breck caught a name that made him jerk up his head. Fisher Tay—of the

33

Box T Ranch—the man who had sworn Breck had killed Tom Stamper.

"What has Fish Tay got to do with this business?" he called out.

There was a smothered curse, a jeering laugh from the spokesman.

"None of yore affair, Allen," came his sullen response. "We was just sort o' figgerin' that mebbe yuh'd like to know who really *did* kill young Tom Stamper."

"I'm listening," Breck called back. "Want to bargain, do you?"

"You git the idee right quick," admired the unseen spokesman. "It's like this, feller. You hand us the gal—an' we'll spill what we know about young Stamper—"

"Go to the devil!" shouted Breck furiously. He flung a shot in the direction of the unseen man. There was an answering groan, a sudden silence, then a stealthy rustle in the thick brush. Breck flung another shot. A man sprang into view, ran frantically up the slope and vanished behind a thicket of prickly pear.

Breck got to his feet. He knew that his last bullet had scored a hit. The fleeing man was the lone survivor of the murderous trio.

He wanted that man badly. He wanted to question him—force the truth from him.

"Wait here," he told Jane curtly. He hurried up the slope.

Almost instantly the whine of a bullet greeted him. Breck dodged to cover. The man was on the alert—desperate.

Reluctantly Breck surrendered his purpose to take the man alive. For the girl's sake he could not afford the risk of a bullet. Jane would be left helpless, at the man's mercy, of which there would be none. The scoundrel could carry the news to old Val Stamper, he reflected grimly. Val Stamper would soon hear that Breck Allen was back on the range—and on the warpath.

Presently, the sound of iron-shod hoofs on the flinty stones told him the survivor was making good his escape.

He went cautiously up the slope, to the ridge Cisco had failed to reach, and caught a glimpse of the fleeing rider before a bend in the ravine hid him from view.

Cisco was dead, he saw. The man's vicious face was unfamiliar. The second man, lying in the brush, he recognized as a former Circle B rider. Breck had forgotten the man's name. He had been discharged from the outfit under suspicion of rustling. It came to Breck's mind as he stared down at the pain-distorted face, that this dead thing had been a boon companion of shiftless Fish Tay of the Box T.

He went gloomily back to Jane, wondering vaguely if it was from Fisher Tay he could wrest the truth about the killing of Tom Stamper. It was possible that the Box T man had himself slain Tom.

"The war is over," he told the girl briefly. "We'll borrow a horse—to take the place of your pinto."

She was jubilant, eager to be away from the spot.

"Poor Aunt Sally!" she worried. "She'll be frantic. I hope she didn't hear the shooting."

Breck thought not. Mexican Wells was a good four or five miles away, he pointed out.

He turned one of the remaining horses loose and led the other one back to Jane. A fine black gelding. Breck remembered Aunt Sally had mentioned that one of the men was riding a black horse. He called the girl's attention to the brand.

"What do you call *that?*"

Jane nodded. "It's a horseshoe," she said in a low voice.

"Mr. Stamper owns the Horseshoe," he reminded curtly.

She nodded again, was silent.

They rode down the long slope toward the Arroyo Seco, followed by the dead Cisco's horse.

"You've made a good trade," Breck said, eyeing the black approvingly.

"I wouldn't keep him for all the world," shuddered the girl. She gave him a sideways glance. He saw the hesitant question in her eyes.

"You're wondering about me," he guessed.

"That man"—she hesitated—"said something about you and—and the sheriff—"

"They thought I killed Tom Stamper—seven years ago," Breck told her frankly. "I didn't."

"I'm sure you didn't!" cried Jane.

"*Gracias, Señorita!*" His eyes twinkled at her.

"The name, *Señor*, is Tallant—Jane Tallant." She looked up at him, and Breck saw that her eyes were the same midnight blue he had glimpsed when he picked her up from the dying pinto. "I have the queerest feeling about you," she said in a low voice. "I seem to have known you always. I suppose," she philosophized, "it breaks down the barriers when people go through what you and I have just been through together." She gave him a faint smile. "We've lived a lifetime together, these last few hours. I feel that we have known each other a thousand years."

"I think I understand," Breck said.

"You saved my life," the girl went on soberly. "Those men were planning to murder me." She reached out a small brown hand. "Shake, Mister Breck Allen—it's *Jane*—to you—" She gave him a misty-eyed smile. "We're *friends*."

"*Gracias*," he repeated.

They gravely shook hands.

"It's *Breck*—to you, Jane—"

Their laughter rose happily above the clatter of hoofs. It was good to be alive—and death had reached so closely for them.

Chapter Three

The Professor's Diary

Early sunlight touched the brown foothill slopes beyond the adobe wall at the end of the garden, when Jane stepped from her room out to the patio gallery. In the far distance she could see the high ridge of the Panamints, already veiled behind a thin haze of heat.

There was a curious expression in Jane's eyes as she moved slowly among beds of bright-colored flowers. This rambling old ranch-house with its quaint walled garden was Breck Allen's home, and she and her aunt were Breck Allen's guests.

It was an amazing situation, reflected the girl. She had not gotten over the surprise of finding herself actually taking refuge at the Circle B Ranch. She had been accusing the Circle B outfit of the cowardly attempts to oust her from Mexican Wells. The coming of Breck Allen—the desperate affair on the bleak slopes below the Painted Canyon, had indicated a motive more sinister than a mere desire to stampede an unwanted settler from Mexican Wells.

The cold-blooded attempt to murder Jane had been too much for Aunt Sally. The old lady had hysterically insisted they agree to Breck's suggestion that she should temporarily abandon the lonely desert homestead. Under their double urgings, Jane had reluctantly consented, reassured by Breck's promise to send men from the ranch to guard Mexican Wells from trespassers.

Jane's eyes shadowed as she recalled the evening of their arrival at the old ranch. Breck's father was not there to make them welcome. For more than a week the owner of the Circle B had lain in his grave, shot from his horse by an unknown assassin.

Voices in the yard beyond the patio gate broke into her thoughts. Breck's quiet tones—the deeper rumble of grizzled Jim Hawker.

"It's an awful risk, Breck, you ridin' in to that town. Val Stamper's the big boss of Calico—"

"I've promised the sheriff to be there, Jim," the girl heard the younger man say in a dogged voice. "We'll start about noon. Things can't go on like this. It's time for a showdown with Val Stamper."

"Reckon you're right, son. I'll tell the boys—"

Jane could hear the foreman clattering off toward the corrals. The gate latch clicked and Breck was suddenly smiling at her.

"You're up early!" He closed the gate and moved to where she stood by the old stone fountain.

"I'm restless," Jane confessed. "I want to *do* something!" She gestured. "It's lovely here at this old place, and you have been so kind to us—but I have work to do—" She sank down on the bench by the side of the little pool and stared unhappily at the misty outline of distant Telescope Peak.

Breck eyed her curiously, brown fingers busy with tobacco and cigarette papers. She had discarded the cowboy clothes for a short linen skirt and blouse. Breck found himself approving the change. The girl was extraordinarily attractive, he suddenly realized. The tom-boyishness had gone—with the doffing of the dusty overalls. Jane was more than pretty. She was charming and beautiful.

Her dark blue eyes met his absorbed look.

"You probably think I'm quite crazy—coming out to this desert country—to Mexican Wells," she went on a bit resentfully.

He sat down on the bench. "I wouldn't say that, Jane—" Breck shook his head. "I've an idea that you had a mighty good reason for going to Mexican Wells—"

"I had!" declared the girl.

"There's nothing there to make the place worth wasting time and risking death to possess," Breck pointed out. "You must have had some powerful motive. I'll admit that I am puzzled."

Jane nodded. "I don't blame you for being puzzled. I'd be crazy to really believe I could make a home—a living in that barren and savage desert country." She paused, musing gaze on the hazy pinnacle of Telescope Peak towering above the sunbaked floor of Death Valley.

"We'll admit that your motive for pretending to homestead Mexican Wells has nothing to do with raising cattle or corn or grain," Breck said. He gave her a grave smile. "I'm not trying to pry into your affairs."

"You have a right to know," Jane told him in a low voice. "Aunt Sally and I owe you our lives. Those men planned to murder both of us—that day." She shivered, gave him a faint smile. "I don't want to be a mystery to you, Breck. We went through a lot together—that afternoon on the slopes below Painted Canyon. Those hours—when death reached so near to us, brought us very close to each other." Jane's small brown hand went out to him. "Don't you remember, Breck? We shook hands on a pact of friendship that afternoon—"

Breck's strong fingers closed over her out-stretched hand. "We're fighting this thing to a finish, together, Jane," he assured her a bit grimly. "We are friends, fighting shoulder to shoulder. I've an odd hunch," he went on musingly, "that there is a connection between the attempt to murder you and my father's murder—"

"It doesn't make sense," argued Jane. "There is no possible reason why my troubles could be linked with the Circle B Ranch."

"We seem to have the same enemies," Breck muttered.

"I don't understand!" Jane's tone was startled.

"I refer to the Horseshoe Ranch—the man who owns it. Those men who tried to murder you—all the other men who threatened you were Val Stamper's riders. Their horses wore the Horse-shoe iron."

Jane shook her head doubtfully. "I can't believe such dreadful things of old Mr. Stamper," she declared. She studied Breck's glowering face thoughtfully. "You don't seem to like Mr. Stamper."

"Stamper and his Horseshoe outfit have fought the Circle B for years," Breck told her. "Because of his hatred, his wish to humiliate and disgrace the Allens, Stamper had me framed for killing his son."

"I think I understand," murmured the girl. "A range war—one of those terrible cattle-country feuds—"

"You've said it," Breck's tone was harsh. "A range war—a fight to the finish. Apparently the finish of the old Circle B, unless I do something about it."

"You will," averred the girl stoutly. "You are not the sort of man who runs away—"

"*Gracias.*" Breck grinned. "There's plenty fight left in the old Circle B. I'm telling Val Stamper this evening there is still an Allen in the saddle."

"That's the talk," smiled Jane. "That is real *man* talk!"

"I can't figure this Mexican Wells business," puzzled Breck. "Val Stamper's been after the place for years. He even offered my father ten thousand dollars in cash to vacate the range between the Arroyo Seco and the Cactus Hills." Breck chuckled. "The only reason Dad didn't grab the money was that he couldn't bear the thought of giving Val Stamper what he wanted." He eyed the girl curiously. "Mexican Wells isn't worth a hoot, except as a round-up camp, which deepens the mystery about yourself. Why do you want Mexican Wells?"

"I was going to explain," Jane said. Her face had paled. "Perhaps you have heard of a Professor Tallant—John Alcott Tallant—"

"Seems to me I have," muttered Breck. He frowned. "Read something years ago in a Dallas paper about him . . . some sort of scientist who mysteriously disappeared." Breck sat up and looked at the girl with startled eyes. "*Tallant!* That's *your* name—"

Jane nodded. "He was my father—an archeologist. It is because of him that I came to Mexican Wells."

"I remember!" exclaimed Breck. "He was lost somewhere in Death Valley."

"I've never been sure," Jane said in a troubled tone. Her gaze went again to the distant Panamints.

"I have come to believe that there was foul play—that it was not in the Funeral Mountains that my father met his death."

"Why would you be looking for him here—in the Cactus Hills?" puzzled Breck.

"It's nearly seven years ago that he disappeared. I was away at a girls' school—in France." She gestured. "He was always on the move—heading expeditions into the strange places of the world: South America, Abyssinia, Egypt—China. The week before I returned to New York he was on his way to Death Valley."

"What makes you believe you can find trace of him in the Mexican Wells country?" Breck wanted to know.

"It's very strange," Jane said. "Of course, searching parties have been sent out to look for him, but finally all hope was abandoned. They say that Death Valley holds its secrets. It's a weird place—"

"It's hell's back yard," agreed Breck. "What happened to revive your hope—bring you to Mexican Wells on the trail?"

"It's very strange," repeated the girl. "I'd entirely given up hope, but a few months ago an old friend of my father wrote to me from Shoshone. He sent me this—" She drew a crumpled piece of paper from the pocket of her brief skirt. "It's a page from my father's diary—"

Breck studied it curiously, a single sheet torn

from a notebook and riddled with tiny holes that in places partly obliterated the crabbed, precise writing.

". . . and saw Pete again . . . quaint old character . . . prospecting for years . . . and sure it's . . . Lost Lode and . . . investigate . . . Horseshoe Lode and Pete says . . . break camp . . . Furnace Creek . . . tomorrow . . . Bad Water . . . with Pete . . . two days . . . Painted Canyon . . . Exciting . . . Pete suspicious . . . thinks we are being trailed . . ."

"It's father's handwriting," Jane said.

"How did this friend get hold of it?" puzzled Breck. "It's undoubtedly a page from the professor's diary."

"A prospector found it in an abandoned cabin in the Funeral Mountains," Jane explained. "You can see it's been badly chewed by rats. The prospector said there was no sign of the rest of the diary. Just this one page, stuck in a crack between the boards."

"I wonder why this prospector gave it to your friend," mused Breck. "It refers plainly to the lost Horseshoe Lode. It's curious the prospector didn't keep the secret for himself."

"The man was very ill, dying," Jane said. "Dr. Wingate was making a lone search for some trace of my father and camped overnight with this man . . . found him dying and tried to help him. The man was grateful . . . gave him the scrap of diary."

Breck nodded. "You've read all this—carefully?"

"Of course!" Her eyes widened. "I know every word by heart—"

"Haven't you noticed something?" His tone was significant.

Jane stared at him. He could see those few precisely-penned words shaping in her mind. Her eyes dilated and she sprang to her feet.

"Why—of course! The Horseshoe Lode!" Her face paled. "The Horseshoe . . . the name of Mr. Stamper's ranch . . . his brand—"

Breck's eyes were bleak. "Perhaps it explains why Mr. Stamper is so interested in Mexican Wells—the Painted Canyon," he said quietly. "Perhaps Mr. Stamper could give you news of your missing father—if we press him—"

She looked at him wildly. Breck could see the quickened beat of her heart under the thin blouse.

"Take it easily," he counseled. "It's time for cool thought—"

"I heard you talking to your foreman," interrupted Jane. Her eyes were very bright. "You told him you were riding to Calico—"

"I am," admitted Breck grimly. "I'm wanting to ask Val Stamper a few questions—"

"I'm going with you," broke in the girl fiercely, "*I* have some questions I want Val Stamper to answer. I'm riding to Calico with you, Breck Allen!"

Chapter Four

The Sheriff of Calico

Sheriff Clem Sorrel thoughtfully contemplated the fat silver watch in the palm of his big hand.

It lacked a few minutes of four o'clock.

The sheriff grunted, looked regretfully at a catalogue lying on the battered desk and slowly returned the ancient timepiece to its accustomed pocket.

"Andy," he said, "I'll be steppin' over to the bank."

His short, bow-legged deputy nodded. "Val'll shore blow up when he hears the news," he prophesied. "He'll be plenty peeved at yuh, Clem."

The sheriff nodded absently, his attention apparently on the highly-colored catalogue in front of him.

"Andy," he said again, "if them rose cuttin's come in on the stage, you be shore an' put 'em in the shade an' give 'em water."

"You bet," promised the deputy. He eyed his chief quizzically as the latter slowly put the catalogue in a drawer of the desk. Sheriff Sorrel was always deliberate in his movements, except when it was necessary to beat some desperado

48

to the first shot. His lightning speed at such moments was legendary.

"You shore think a heap of yore rose garden," Andy grinned. "You've about wore that catalogue to pieces."

"Martha likes 'em about the house," returned the sheriff placidly.

"You take the cake," marveled the deputy. "If I didn't know yuh for the damn nerviest sheriff in the state of Nevada I'd say yuh was a ol' woman —the way you putter round with them roses." Andy's affectionate tone belied an implied scorn of his chief's hobby.

"I'll be steppin' over to the bank," repeated the sheriff mildly. He uncoiled his long, gaunt frame from the decrepit chair and buckled on a gun-holster. His wide shoulders were a trifle stooped under his nearly seventy years, but the blue eyes in his kindly, weathered face were singularly alert and keen.

"Don't forget to give them rose cuttin's a mite o' water, Andy," he reminded as he turned leisurely to the door.

The sunlight was yellowing in Calico's dusty main street. Evening shadows were already pushing up the low hills in the west.

The sheriff paused and stared intently at the shadowed slopes. What he saw seemed to satisfy him. He moved on across the dusty street, an odd, speculative gleam in the blue eyes.

Mat Haley was sitting on his hotel porch, enjoying the late afternoon's cooling breeze. Mat owned the Haley House, the town's one hostelry. He was a wiry little man, with shrewd, kindly eyes, and like the veteran sheriff he wore a drooping grizzled mustache.

"Howdy, Clem." The hotel man straightened up in the comfortable rocker. "What's the news from the ranch?" He wagged his head. "Bad business! Shore was one square-shootin' *hombre*—old Breck Allen. Any idee who done the killin', Clem?"

"We're workin' on it, Mat," was the sheriff's noncommittal reply.

"Tough deal for young Breck—comin' home after all these years, an' findin' the old man murdered—shot in the back from ambush." Mat Haley's shrewd eyes unsuccessfully probed the sheriff's inscrutable face. "Ain't yuh dug up no clues, Clem?"

"Too soon to talk, Mat." Sheriff Sorrel's gaze was on the shadowed hills beyond the town. "Looks like Jim Hawker an' his outfit, ridin' in to town—"

The hotel man stared up the street. "Reckon you're right. Jim an' the Circle B boys always put up at my place—" Mat rose spryly from the rocker. "Wong will want to know the boys will be in for supper—"

The veteran law officer nodded, moved on

toward the bank. Bart Cordy hailed him from across the street.

"How's the roses bloomin', ol' longhorn?"

The saloon man laughed disagreeably.

Sheriff Sorrel continued his leisurely progress to the Calico Valley Stockman's Bank. He was proof against Bart Cordy's derision. The saloon man's ambition to be sheriff was no secret. He was campaigning for the office—with the fall election less than three months away and Val Stamper's money behind him.

A man rode into the street, Fish Tay, on his claybank horse. The sheriff halted reluctantly at the man's hail.

"Want to see yuh a moment," grinned the big Box T man, reining his horse.

"What about, Fish?" queried the sheriff mildly.

"That there ree-ward—for bringin' yuh the tip 'bout young Breck Allen. I was the first to tell yuh he was back—" There was an avid gleam in the man's evil eyes. "Five thousand cash for Breck Allen—dead or alive. That's what Val Stamper said. It's been posted up in his bank for years."

"Reckon yuh must talk to Val about it, Fish," the sheriff said dryly. "There's no reward hung up in my office."

"It's up to you to tell Val that I was the one to give yuh the tip," grumbled Fish Tay.

"I'm headin' for the bank now," the sheriff told him. "I'll speak to Val about that reward." His long, gaunt frame drifted on up the street and vanished into the small, new brick building that stood aloof from its neighbors on a corner lot. Neat lettering in gold leaf on the two plate glass windows informed the public that this was:

THE CALICO VALLEY
STOCKMAN'S BANK
Val Stamper
PRESIDENT

Sheriff Sorrel eased his long frame into a chair by the desk. His smile was friendly.

"Well, Val? You said for me to drop in round about four o'clock. What's on yore mind?"

"You don't need to ask me!" snapped the banker. "You know well enough what's on my mind, Clem."

The sheriff gazed at him thoughtfully. Val Stamper, financier and cattleman, owner of the big Horseshoe Ranch, was perhaps in his middle sixties. He was small, and thin to the verge of being skinny. His enemies, and they were not few, spoke of him as "that old buzzard." There was a decided vulture-like look about Val Stamper, with his long, flat, bald head and the beaked nose drawing down over straight, thin lips, and the shiny, black, unblinking eyes.

"You know what's on my mind," he repeated angrily.

"Maybe so," murmured the sheriff. He stared musingly at a poster that adorned the wall near the street door. It was faded, and age-yellowed, printed in big type. Sheriff Sorrel could read the top line easily from where he sat.

The sheriff's face hardened as he stared at that ancient poster.

$5000.

REWARD
DEAD OR ALIVE

"Breck Allen's been back a week," fumed the banker. "You haven't made a move. Why isn't he in jail?"

"What do you use for a heart, Val?" The sheriff's voice was thin. "Expect me to arrest that boy—and his father scarcely cold in his grave?"

"Old Breck is buried now," grumbled Stamper. "No sense for you to wait any longer." His voice tightened and he pounded the desk with bony, clenched fist. "I want young Breck Allen in jail. He's going to hang for killing my son!"

The old sheriff looked at him steadily.

"Who's going to hang for shootin' his dad in the back?" he asked softly.

"That's your business," grumbled the cattleman-banker. "And it's your business to arrest young Breck—or we'll have a new sheriff in this county."

"I'm shore of one thing." Sheriff Sorrel's tone

was grim. "Some *hombre* is goin' to swing for murderin' old Breck Allen." He got up slowly from the chair and went deliberately to the ancient reward poster.

"This thing has been hanging here too long, Val," he said. There was the sound of tearing paper.

"Damn you, Sorrel!" The banker sprang to his feet. "What's the idee—destroyin' that reward notice?"

Sheriff Sorrel flung the balled shreds of paper into a wastebasket.

"Listen to me, Val," he said sternly. "I never did believe young Breck shot your son. You've had it in for the Allens for years—or you'd have given Breck a chance to tell his story about that shootin'. Instead of playin' fair, you fixed to have the boy lynched. 'Twas me that got him away—told him to git out of the country, an' 'twas me that wrote to him and said for him to come back. I promised him my protection. He's back—to clear his name of that charge of murder you laid against him." The sheriff's voice deepened. "I'm keepin' that promise! You don't lay a finger on that boy till he's had his chance to prove he never shot Tom."

"He's as guilty as hell," sneered Stamper. His skinny frame relaxed into the swivel chair, black, unwinking eyes stared furiously at the granite-faced law officer. "I'm warning you,

Clem—if you don't clap young Breck Allen behind the bars, he'll swing from a tree before another sun-rise."

"I reckon not," Sheriff Sorrel said softly. He appeared to be listening to the sudden clatter of horses' hoofs in the street. "I reckon not, Val," he repeated. "Breck is in town now—for a show-down with you on this business—"

"Breck Allen—in town!" Val Stamper's bald head poked forward on skinny neck. "Listen to me, Clem! I want Breck inside that jail of yours! If he didn't shoot my son, he can prove it to a jury!"

"A fat chance Breck would have with your packed jury—with that drunken bum you put in as judge, Val." Sheriff Sorrel's keen blue eyes blazed. "I've promised Breck his chance. He won't git no chance in jail—nor from your jury an' judge—"

"You've gone loony, Clem," grumbled the banker. His bony fist pounded the desk. "We need a new sheriff in this county!"

Sheriff Sorrel grinned. "You'd shore be boss of yore dunghill, Clem, with Bart Cordy sittin' in the sheriff's office an' doin' yore dirty work—"

"I'll have you indicted," fumed Calico's most prominent citizen. "I don't take that sort of talk from you—or anybody. I'll have your star—if it means appealing to the Supreme Court of this state."

"I'm talkin' plenty more to yuh, Val," the

sheriff went on placidly. "Listen close, for yore own good. Breck Allen is on the prod, mister—"

Something like fear flickered in the banker's cold, unwinking eyes.

"You know what I mean, Val," continued the sheriff in his deep voice. "The week before Breck got home to the ranch, his dad was shot in the back—killed by a skulkin' bushwhacker—"

The banker gestured nervously. "I don't know a thing about that killing, Clem—"

The old sheriff's blue eyes hardened. "I'm not accusin' *you,* Val—" His deep voice rumbled on. "You an' yore Horseshoe outfit have always been on the warpath 'gainst the Allens—"

"Breck figgered he owned the whole damn country," grumbled the baron of Horseshoe Ranch. He shook his head sadly. "It was a shock—to hear of his death—his murder, Clem. I've fought Breck and his Circle B tooth and nail for years. He gave me as good as I gave him, but we always made it a fair and square fight. There's been gunplay—but not *murder.*"

"I ain't so certain about it," demurred the sheriff. "I can name five Circle B men, not includin' old Breck. All of 'em bushwhacked—killed—"

Val Stamper stiffened in his big swivel chair.

"Meanin' just what?"

"Meanin' that young Breck is in town to ask you some questions." Sheriff Sorrel's angular frame lifted from the chair. "He'll be in to see you *pronto*, Val. Him—and Jim Hawker—an' the Circle B boys—" He moved with his deliberate stride to the street door.

"Clem!" There was panic in the banker's voice. "I want Breck put in jail! I'm boss in this town—"

"I'm still sheriff of Calico County," drawled the veteran law officer.

"I'll have your star," promised the angry man. "You'll hear from Kirk Bannion about this—"

"Here's yore dog now," grinned the sheriff.

Kirk Bannion pushed through the door.

"Looks like the Circle B outfit has come to town to celebrate—or something," he announced. His sleepy brown eyes flickered at the law officer. "Hello, Clem! How are the roses?"

"Doin' nicely, thank yuh, Kirk." There was frost in Sheriff Sorrel's voice, a frank distaste in the look he gave the suave-tongued lawyer.

"Doddering old fool," grumbled the banker as the door closed behind the law officer's long, gaunt frame. "We've got to get rid of him, Kirk."

Kirk Bannion eased his elegant person into the chair vacated by the sheriff. He moved with a panther-like grace, a tall, supple man in the early forties, with the olive complexion of one born below the border. The hair under flat-brimmed white hat was a shiny black, and his teeth showed even and white under a thin jet mustache. He wore burnished brown boots, whipcord riding breeches and a white silk shirt with a flowing crimson tie.

"What's in the wind, Val?" His sleepy brown eyes fixed with peculiar intentness on the banker's worried face.

"Young Breck Allen's in the wind," snarled the old man. "He's in this cowtown now—if you want to know!"

Kirk Bannion's long, dexterous fingers toyed with a cigar. "Ah," he murmured. "The young man on the tall gray horse would be this Breck *hombre*." There was an odd absence of mirth in his lazy smile. "Something of an *hombre*—this young Breck Allen, I'd say—"

"He's a killer," fumed the banker. "He shot my boy. I want him in jail—a rope round his neck—"

"Well?" There was a sneer in the lawyer's eyes as he stared at his client. "Isn't your sheriff on the job?"

"Clem refuses to lift a hand against him . . . says he's promised Breck a chance to prove he didn't shoot Tom."

"I fear that old longhorn needs a stiff lesson," murmured Kirk Bannion. "We need a man like Bart Cordy in our business, eh, Val?" He lit the cigar and gazed reflectively at the other man. "What do you suppose brings Breck Allen to town? That Tallant girl is with him."

Old Val Stamper stiffened in his big swivel chair. "The Tallant girl?" he croaked. "You mean that Mexican Wells nester?"

"The same young lady." Bannion's smile again was oddly mirthless. "She and Breck Allen will be safe enough in this town of yours tonight, Val. Jim Hawker and about every good fighting man of the Circle B are along with them."

"I don't savvy this business," worried old Stamper. "How do you suppose Breck and this girl got together?"

"I'd like to know the answer," Kirk Bannion said in his purring voice. He shrugged immaculate silk-clad shoulders. "Al Roan and his outfit are due in town this evening. Shouldn't be surprised if Al Roan has some news—"

Val Stamper scowled. "There'll likely be trouble," he grumbled. He got up from his chair and reached for his hat. "Kirk—keep an eye open for Al. Send him over to my house the minute he gets in with the outfit—"

"What's your rush?" interrupted the lawyer. "If you're afraid your Horseshoe outfit will have trouble with that Circle B bunch, why don't you stick around and look after things?"

The banker pulled on his battered felt hat. "I ain't feeling well," he mumbled. "Clem says Breck Allen figgers on having a showdown with me, and I ain't in a mood to talk to the skunk— or to that Mexican Wells nester—if you want to know." He motioned to the door. "Get movin', Kirk. I'm going out the back way. Don't want to risk running into Breck. I want him behind the bars—when I talk to him."

Kirk Bannion nodded and got out of his chair. Cynical amusement lurked in his sleepy eyes. He had learned much about Val Stamper during the two years he had been the banker's legal adviser.

"*Adios, Señor*," he murmured politely. "I will give Al Roan your message. In the meantime we must hope that the streets of Calico will not be shocked by the crash of six-guns tonight."

Chapter Five

A Bald-Faced Horse

The Circle B contingent off-saddled at Sam Horner's Livery & Feed Stables.

"No tellin' when hell will bust loose in this town, once the news gets round you are here," grizzled Jim Hawker told Breck. "We want the broncs in good shape if trouble comes on the prod."

Sam Horner eyed them askance. He was a lean, leather-faced man with grayish mouse-colored hair and pale blue eyes.

"Hi, Breck!" He offered a limp hand. "Ain't seen yuh for a coon's age." The liveryman stared with undisguised curiosity at Jane. "Went an' got married while yuh was gone, huh?" He grinned, showed tobacco-stained teeth under his ragged mustache.

"Not married," Breck said curtly. "Miss Tallant is a neighbor." He reddened under the girl's amused smile. "You take care of things here," he told Jim Hawker. "I'll show Jane over to Mat's place."

The Circle B foreman nodded. "No need for you to wait, Breck," he agreed. "Reckon Miss Jane shore craves to rest up after five hours in

61

the saddle." He drew Breck to one side. "I'm not thinking much of this Horner *hombre*," he said in a low voice. "Sam's a Val Stamper man an' cunnin' as a coyote, but we ain't got no choice. It's let the broncs get a feed here—or have 'em stand in the street."

"Leave a couple of the boys on guard," suggested Breck.

"Shore will," grunted the veteran foreman. "Well—see you later at Mat's." He disappeared into the dim interior of the long barn.

Breck and Jane crossed over to the board sidewalk. Sunset fires flared over the sawtooth ridge of the Cactus Hills, made pale gold mist of the dust that lifted in the wake of a cavalcade of horsemen riding into Calico's main street. Breck's eyes narrowed. He suspected the identity of those approaching riders.

Jane sensed his perturbation.

"The Horseshoe outfit," she murmured.

He nodded, was aware of an odd pleasure and satisfaction as he met her cool, unafraid little smile. She was a girl to ride the river with—this Jane Tallant.

Seven years had made small change in Calico. Save for the new brick bank building, the little cowtown's dusty main street was as Breck remembered. Dan Smeed's blacksmith shop, adjacent to Horner's livery barn, Dan busy at his forge; one hand working the bellows, his other hand skillfully tonguing the white-hot metal that soon would be fitted to the hoofs of the cow pony drooping inside the shop.

The skinny blacksmith looked up, met Breck's friendly smile with an astonished stare that turned to a scowl. Sparks geysered up from the forge and the blacksmith's gaze went back to the horseshoe in the glowing coals.

The man's frank enmity shocked Breck. Dan Smeed had been a friend in the old days.

They passed Guttersen's General Merchandise Emporium. Sol Guttersen, florid of face, blue pencil in the pink ear under a shock of white hair, was watching from his doorway. With a startled look in his eyes, the old merchant hurriedly turned his back.

It was the same all the way up the street. Scowls and lowering faces, or obvious reluctance to indicate any friendliness for the man who had dared to defy the vengeance of Val Stamper.

Old Mat Haley was the exception. The hotel keeper beamed.

"Lad! 'Tis a grand day to see Breck Allen's boy again!" He pumped Breck's hand warmly. " 'Tis welcome ye are, son." Mat transferred his attention to Jane.

"Ye'll be wantin' to clean up after the ride in from the ranch. I'll show ye to your room, an' Teresa'll have a hot tub for ye by the time ye're ready."

"I'll remember you in my prayers," smiled the girl. To Breck she whispered, "Be careful . . . I saw the way people looked at you. This town is dangerous—"

"I'll be right careful," he promised solemnly, secretly pleased at her concern for his safety. His eyes twinkled. "See you later—in the dining room, Jane."

The girl's trim figure disappeared into the hall. Mat Haley watched her with appreciative eyes.

"Nice young woman," he admired; "trig and pretty as they come." He gave Breck a shrewd smile and went to look after his guest.

Breck turned back to the street for a closer view of the horsemen now drawing rein in front of the Outpost saloon. Sheriff Sorrel lifted a beckoning hand from his office door across the street.

"I'd keep away from there, son," he said gravely as Breck joined him. "That's Al Roan, and his Horseshoe bunch." The sheriff's tone was worried. "Shore tough—you two outfits in town at the same time. You'd better warn your boys to keep away from Bart Cordy's place."

Breck grinned. "You know cowboys, Clem. They don't take much to apron strings."

Sheriff Sorrel nodded gloomily. "Cowboys don't shy away from trouble," he admitted. "Not them salty fellers on *your* payroll."

The sun sank below the Cactus Hills, left a

64

crimson stain along the horizon. The lights and shadows of eventide flushed the slopes, filled the drab street with a softening glow. As if in response to this more gracious mood, life began to flow in the town. Women and girls appeared on the planked sidewalks, stood gossiping in front of Guttersen's store. The stage was due, with the mail, and Guttersen was postmaster.

Jim Hawker and his men drew up the street from Horner's barn. Hawker paused to speak to the sheriff.

"See Al Roan an' his fellers are in town," he said. "Tough luck!"

Sorrel nodded. He was watching three riders drifting up the street.

"Bowie Smith," he muttered. "You'll remember him, Breck. Owns the Lazy S place. Those other fellers will be the Gorman brothers, Bill an' Ned . . . got small spreads down in the south fork of the Calico."

Breck's eyes questioned him. He sensed there was something on the sheriff's mind.

"I sent for 'em to come an' have a talk with you," Sorrel went on. "This cow stealin' has got 'em plumb wild . . . somethin' is got to be done plenty quick. They knew how old Breck Allen stood about this rustlin', but he's gone, an' they aim to find out how *you* stand . . . if you'll throw in with 'em against this gang o' cow-stealers an' brand-blotters."

"There's no question how I stand," Breck told him grimly.

"We'll get together in your room, tonight," the sheriff said. "Hey—where you goin', son?"

"Want to have a look at that bald-faced horse—" Breck nodded, moved away.

Jim Hawker's eyes signaled Johnny and Dusty. It was their job to stick close to Breck. It was significant of Johnny Wing and Dusty Rodes that each wore two guns, tied low. They were not "killers," but few men could get their guns into action quite as fast as these two boyish-faced cowboys.

Kirk Bannion pushed through the crowd lined up at the long bar and button-holed Bart Cordy. The sleepiness had gone from his brown eyes. They smouldered angrily.

"Bart!" The lawyer gestured at a dark-faced Mexican idling with a pack of cards at a corner table. "Tell Ramon to fork his bronc and get out of this town—"

The saloon man listened attentively as Bannion whispered something. The lawyer turned back to the street door.

Breck was staring at the cow ponies drooping at the long hitch-rail. Lounging near the wall were Johnny Wing and Dusty Rodes. Kirk Bannion paused, gave Breck a lazy-eyed glance, and moved on across the street toward the Haley House. Breck's gaze followed him, returned to the bald-faced sorrel that had attracted his attention. He would know that bald-faced horse anywhere. But he was not certain of the man who had ridden the animal that afternoon on the slopes below the Painted Canyon. To look for the man in the saloon would be futile. He must wait for the horse to be claimed.

Kirk Bannion reached the wide porch of the Haley House and dropped into a chair. A look told him that Breck was sauntering down the street toward the sheriff's office. The two young punchers were arguing in front of the saloon's swing doors. The youth with the straw-colored hair seemed to be in favor of Jose's *cantina,* an adobe building, half hidden in a grove of umbrella trees several hundred yards up the street. He lifted a loud voice.

"Come on, feller! I shore crave a *tortilla*—"

"Never did see an *hombre* so loco about Mex food as you, Johnny," grumbled his dark-faced companion.

The two moved on, wrangling good-naturedly. Kirk Bannion's eyes glinted satisfaction.

Three horsemen passed the hotel and made for Horner's livery barn. The tall bearded man gave the lawyer a stony look. Bowie Smith, of the Lazy S, Kirk Bannion recognized. He had recently filed suit against the man to collect a note held by Val Stamper's bank.

Several men pushed out of the saloon. One

of them, a Mexican, darted a quick glance at Breck, strolling toward the sheriff's office. With a muttered word to his companions, the man twitched loose the horse-hair tie rope that secured the bald-faced sorrel and slid lithely into the saddle. In a moment he was riding away at a jog trot in the direction taken by the two cowboys on their way to Jose's *cantina*.

Johnny Wing's glance slid over his shoulder.

"It's the baldy bronc," he murmured.

"The Mex forkin' him will be the *hombre* the boss is lookin' for," Dusty Rodes opined after a brief stare.

Stern purpose erased the happy-go-lucky smiles from their young faces. There was a sudden narrowing of the eyes. Too late the bald-faced sorrel's rider saw his danger, drew the horse to a quick halt.

"Get his smoke-pot, Dusty," Johnny Wing said. His gun menaced the sullen-eyed man on the horse. "Keep yore hands where I can see 'em, mister."

Dusty Rodes moved in close and deftly removed the Mexican's gun.

"Now yuh can climb down," he said. "Make it snappy," he added. A sudden commotion down the street warned of the need of haste. The Mexican's recent companions were clattering up the sidewalk.

"Get a move on yuh!" snarled Dusty. "Stop them fellers," he said to Johnny Wing.

The latter's gun roared. The clatter of booted feet was suddenly hushed. The Mexican slid from his saddle, and obeying Johnny's curt words, faced down street, his hands above his head.

More men poured from the saloon, milled excitedly in the street. Beyond the crowd loomed the tall figures of Breck Allen and the sheriff. The latter's voice boomed warningly.

"No gun-play, you fellers. I'm takin' charge."

Gun in hand the law officer pushed through the crowd, Breck at his heels. Kirk Bannion got up from his porch chair and watched the scene, an ugly gleam in his eyes.

"What's the trouble?" demanded the sheriff curtly as he panted up.

"Reckon it's up to the boss to tell yuh," grinned Johnny Wing. He fell back to Dusty's side, cold blue eyes alertly watching the men trailing up from the saloon. Breck spoke.

"I'm asking for this man's arrest, Sheriff."

"What's the charge?" Sheriff Sorrel wanted to know. He drooped an eyelid. The story of the afternoon on the slopes below the Painted Canyon was already known to him. "What for you want me to throw Ramon Matute in jail, Breck?"

"For attempted murder," answered the Circle B man curtly.

The old sheriff nodded. "Yuh kin put yore hands down, Ramon," he said softly; and as the

Mexican obeyed there was the sudden click of
steel. Ramon's face went a sickly green. He stared
with frightened, sullen eyes at his manacled
wrists.

An angry bellow came from the saloon door
and a burly man shoved furiously through the
silently watching group on the sidewalk.

"What's the idee, Sorrel?" The newcomer's
voice choked with rage. "What are you arrestin'
Ramon for?"

"For attempted murder, Roan—"

"Turn him loose!" shouted the Horseshoe
foreman. "I ain't standin' for it, Sorrel!"

"Reckon not, Al," said the sheriff in a mild
tone. His glance raked the scowling men gathered
behind the Horseshoe man's back. "I'm advisin'
yuh to keep yore boys peaceable," he warned.

Al Roan hesitated. He was too wise not to
realize that he was in a trap. The derisive look in
Breck's gray eyes told him that he would be
the first to go down if he made a move to pull
his gun. And crouched in various doorways could
be seen the watchful faces of Circle B men,
ready to blast the lives of the Horseshoe gunfighters bunched behind him. He was out-
numbered two to one.

"Val Stamper'll have yore star for this," he said
with an oath.

"In the meantime I'm takin' Ramon over to
the jail," replied Sheriff Sorrel placidly. "Git

70

movin', Ramon. Yuh'll be in time for supper."

"Kirk Bannion will have him out of jail *pronto*," boasted the Horseshoe foreman. He fell back, a glance warning his men not to interfere.

Breck motioned to a Circle B man to take the bald-faced sorrel.

"What you aim to do with that bronc?" snarled Al Roan. "That's a Horseshoe bronc."

"Was Ramon using him on Horseshoe business when he tried to murder Miss Tallant?" Breck's tone was thin. "There were three of 'em riding Horseshoe broncs up there in the Painted Canyon, Roan. Reckon Ramon has told you where you can find Cisco—and the other man—or weren't they up there on your business, mister—"

"I don't git yuh, Allen." Roan's face paled. "No *hombre* named Cisco was ever on the Horseshoe payroll—"

"We'll know more when Ramon does some talking, Roan." The Circle B owner's tone hardened. "Ramon will talk plenty before we finish with him. Shouldn't be surprised if we find out who murdered my father—"

"You're loco," scoffed Roan. "You can't pin that killin' on my outfit, Allen." He darted an uneasy glance at Fish Tay, watching with Bart Cordy from the saloon door.

Breck noticed and registered the look. His face hardened.

"You're loco," repeated the Horseshoe foreman.

71

He stamped angrily away, followed by his hard-faced crew.

Breck smiled at Johnny Wing and Dusty Rodes.

"Good work, boys," he told them. "How about supper?" He chuckled. "Or do you still crave some of Jose's *tortillas*, Johnny?"

They grinned at him.

"That Chinaman Mat has in his kitchen puts up a meal that makes yuh think it's Christmas," Johnny Wing declared earnestly. He smacked his lips. "Boss—the apple pie old Wong turns out of his oven is somethin' to live for—"

Al Roan was conversing in low tones with Kirk Bannion when the trio reached the hotel porch. Jane, refreshed from the hot, dusty ride, appeared in the doorway, her eyes big with excitement. The lawyer looked round as Breck and the two punchers mounted the steps.

"It seems to me you're going off at half cock, Allen," he said aggressively. "You can't throw a man in jail because you think you recognize his horse. I'm Bannion," he added, "Kirk Bannion. I attend to Val Stamper's legal matters."

"You can talk to Sheriff Sorrel about it," Breck told him pleasantly. He turned to Jane.

"Just a moment!" The lawyer smiled protestingly. "Al Roan claims you've had Ramon Matute arrested merely because he was riding a bald-faced sorrel horse. There are hundreds of bald-faced horses, and even if Ramon's horse is the one you saw up at the Painted Canyon, you have no proof that Ramon was riding the animal that afternoon."

"I'd know that horse anywhere," answered Breck coldly. "It's logical to believe that Ramon Matute was one of the three men who tried to murder Miss Tallant."

"I'm sure of it," Jane broke in from the doorway. "My aunt says that three men riding Horseshoe animals were at Mexican Wells that morning. One of them was a Mexican, on a bald-faced sorrel horse."

The lawyer smiled politely. "You are Miss Tallant?" he murmured. "I have heard Della Stamper speak of you," he went on smoothly. "She has been singing your praises." Bannion's eyebrows lifted ironically. "Your aunt's description of these scoundrels—and their horses—still does not prove that Ramon Matute was the Mexican she saw. There are many Mexican *vaqueros* in the Calico country, Miss Tallant."

Doubt grew in the girl's eyes. She gave Breck a worried look. Val Stamper had been very kind to her, she recalled, and Della's friendliness was unfeigned. Kirk Bannion's polite skepticism disturbed her. The lawyer was decidedly attractive —not the sort of man who would take sides with cold-blooded killers.

"Perhaps you made a mistake," she said to

Breck in a low voice. "We mustn't accuse an innocent man, Breck, unless—"

"I have made no mistake." Breck's tone was grim. He looked at the silently attentive Johnny and Dusty. "Go and get your suppers, boys— and don't eat *all* that apple pie."

The two young cowboys grinned at each other sheepishly.

"Reckin we'll wait awhile, boss," Johnny said awkwardly.

Jim Hawker had promised to give them their time if they let Breck out of their sight. The young cattleman grinned.

"I savvy," he said dryly. His gaze returned to the lawyer and the glowering Horseshoe foreman.

"There's no mistake, Bannion," he repeated. "I'd say it's too bad for somebody that Ramon isn't lying up there in the Cactus Hills along with those two friends of his. It was some fight," he mused. "Miss Tallant will tell you about it in court, you and the jury. I killed two of 'em, Bannion; and as I just said, it's going to be too bad for some person—or persons—that I didn't kill Ramon, too."

"What yuh drivin' at?" snarled Al Roan. His hand hovered over gun-butt.

"Don't get excited, mister," warned Johnny Wing.

Roan gave him an ugly look, uncurled his reaching fingers.

"I mean that Ramon will talk—and talk plenty—to save his own skin," explained Breck pleasantly. "Ramon has nothing to lose and everything to gain—by coming across with the true story."

"You're being absurd, Allen," laughed Kirk Bannion. "However, as I am Mr. Stamper's attorney, it's my business to inform him of this matter. Ramon Matute is his employee." He smiled at Jane. "I'll tell Della you are in town, Miss Tallant. I'm sure she will insist that you stay with her while you are here."

"Smooth," muttered Breck, as the lawyer went on his way with Al Roan.

"I think Mr. Bannion is rather nice," protested Jane. "You know, Breck, I really can't bring myself to believe that Della Stamper's father could possibly be mixed up with this business."

"Let's see what Wong has for supper tonight," was Breck's response. "Johnny Wing swears old Wong's apple pie is something to talk about."

Sheriff Sorrel came into the dining room. Bowie Smith was with him. The former paused to speak to Breck.

"Bowie Smith and the others aim to have a talk with you soon as you've had yore supper," he said in a low voice. He frowned, drew down the shade. "Thought you had better sense," he grumbled. "You shouldn't take chances in this cowtown, son."

75

Fear looked from Jane's lovely eyes.

"Oh, Breck," she whispered. "Is it really so bad—" Her troubled glance went to Johnny Wing and Dusty Rodes. She understood now why those wary-eyed young cowboys stayed so close to the man sitting opposite her.

Chapter Six

Two Men Dead

Jim Hawker was the first to rap the agreed signal on Breck's door. Anxiety furrowed the Circle B foreman's weather-bitten visage.

"There's a lot of talk floatin' round this town," he gloomily told Breck. "Al Roan's outfit is red-eyed about this Mexican yuh had the sheriff throw into jail." Jim Hawker wagged his head. "You lost yore wits, it seems to me, Breck. You should have waited till we could have rounded up this *hombre* by his lonesome—once yuh'd spotted him for the man yuh wanted."

Breck stared with some surprise at the veteran cowman.

"That sort of talk doesn't sound like you, Jim."

"Mebbe not," muttered Hawker. "Mebbe you figger I'm losin' my nerve." He smiled faintly. "Don't figger me wrong, Breck. I've been goin' through a lot of hell these last few months. Five good men killed—and then old Breck—shot in the back—"

"That is one reason why we're in this town tonight," Breck said quietly. "You're as keen as I am to get the man who killed my father."

"We worked a lot of cattle together, me an'

him," the foreman said simply. "He was my best friend."

Breck nodded. Jim and old Breck had been close friends as long as he could remember. The prestige of the Circle B was always first with stanch Jim Hawker. It was not personal danger that troubled the grizzled foreman. It was the ranch that worried him—the fear that the existence of the Circle B was threatened by the growing power of their enemies.

"It's like this, Breck," continued Hawker. "You are the last of the Allens. If anything happens to you, it means the finish for the Circle B." He stared at the cigarette between gnarled fingers. "I claim it was a fool play for you to come to this town. This place is Val Stamper's hangout. He's the big boss here—and he's layin' for yuh. There's scarcely a man in Calico that'll stand by yuh—save old Clem Sorrel an' Mat Haley—an' a few ol' timers like 'em. You went an' jumped too soon, Breck."

"Maybe I did," admitted the young man. "I was sort of pushed, Jim. So much has happened—"

He glowered at the door. Footsteps were approaching down the hall. It was true that a lot had happened since his return from exile. He had come home primarily for two reasons. Sheriff Sorrel had written that his father needed him. His other reason was the desire to clear his name as the killer of Tom Stamper. Things

78

had piled up. The mysterious attacks on Jane Tallant—the startling discovery that the old ranch was doomed unless the increasing boldness of the cattle rustlers could be checked. It was in Breck's mind that the various angles of the baffling affair took source from one root. To uncover this root of lawlessness was his business.

Sheriff Sorrel made his appearance, nodded approval at the blankets Breck had draped across the two windows overlooking the street.

"Bowie Smith'll be up in a minute or two," he informed the others. "Bill an' Ned'll trail up quick as they can. Told 'em not to come in a crowd. Might attract notice. No tellin' who's a spy in this town—"

A soft, hesitant rap on the door interrupted the sheriff.

"Jane!" muttered Breck.

He went to the door. The girl beckoned him out to the hall. Her eyes were very bright, he saw.

"Breck! Della's downstairs. She wants me to spend the night with her—"

He frowned. "No!"

Jane interrupted him. "I've thought it over," she said. "I want to go, Breck. It's a chance to learn something. I'm sure to see her father—"

"I don't like you going to Val Stamper's house," Breck continued to demur.

Jane was not to be turned from her purpose. "I'm going," she declared flatly. "Why should *you* do all the work—take all the risks? It's my chance to do something to help. I'll be safe enough at the Stampers'."

Bowie Smith came down the hall. Jane turned hastily to her door.

"*Adios, Señor*—until the morning—" She threw him a smile over her shoulder and closed the door.

The bearded owner of the Lazy S wore an anxious look.

"Don't like the talk that's goin' on down in the street," he told the sheriff somberly. "There's some skunk working up bad feelin' against Breck."

"I've got Andy Hogan watchin' things," reassured the sheriff. "Jim Hawker posted five of his boys in the lobby, and a dozen more fellers on the look-out in the street."

"Breck made a fool play with the Mex *hombre*," grumbled Jim Hawker.

Ned Gorman arrived, and a few moments later, his brother clattered into the room. Breck knew these three cowmen. The Gorman brothers were former Circle B riders who had gone into the cattle business for themselves.

Breck was conscious of a thrill as he studied them. These ranchers were looking to him to lead them, as they had looked to his slain father. The thought stiffened his resolve.

"You do the talkin', Bowie," suggested the sheriff. "Next to the Circle B, your Lazy S outfit has suffered most from this cow stealing."

"We got to do something—an' do it quick," Bowie Smith declared. "There's always been cow stealin'—but not on the scale it is now."

"It's an organized gang," Ned Gorman grumbled. "Fellers, my G Bar G is rustled to the bone. I won't ship a beef this fall."

"Same with me," grunted Bill Gorman. "We're in one hell of a mess, Breck."

"The Circle B is in a worse mess than any of yuh," growled old Jim Hawker. "These skulkin' range wolves don't stop with stealing cows. They're killers. Five of my boys bushwhacked— not to mention poor old Breck Allen."

"An organized gang would mean there's a master mind back of this business," Breck told them. "Any of you got a notion who the king-wolf might be?"

"I've got plenty notions," Bowie Smith answered. "The man I figger's back of this rustlin' don't seem like no king-wolf, though. He's more like an old buzzard—feeding on our rangelands, picking our bones clean."

"You've drawn the picture," muttered Bill Gorman.

"It's going to be a hard thing to prove, Bowie." Breck's tone was grave.

"I reckon you know what I'm drivin' at," answered the bearded Lazy S man.

"Val Stamper?" Breck's face was grim. "The Circle B has been fighting him for years, but it's hard to believe Val would go in for rustling. He has no quarrel with you boys."

"He owns my note for seven thousand," said Bowie Smith bitterly. "If I don't pay him off, he's due to take my ranch."

"He won't renew the note—give you a chance?" queried Breck.

"He won't do nothin'." Bowie Smith swore. "He's set that slick-tongued Bannion shark on me already."

"Who is this Kirk Bannion?" asked Breck for the second time that day. "Where's he from?"

"Never heard where he was from," answered the sheriff. "He's right popular in town. Val Stamper's right bower—and future son-in-law, I reckon."

"He looks Mexican to me," mused Breck. "I'll bet my last chip he wasn't born with the name of Kirk Bannion."

"Come to think of it, Kirk is awful thick with the Mexicans round here." Sheriff Sorrel's tone was thoughtful. "Seen Kirk several times over at Jose Moraga's *cantina*. Can talk Spanish fast as any of 'em."

"He's mighty thick with Al Cordy, too," broke in Ned Gorman. "If Bannion is Val's right bower, that crawlin' sidewinder Cordy shore is Val's left bower. It's a combination that don't set well in my craw," the G Bar G man added darkly.

"Wild guesses won't get us anywhere," observed

Breck. "Just the same we're here to let loose anything that's in our minds. What do you know about Fisher Tay?" he went on. "Ran into Fish the day I got home. I'll bet he carried the news to you, Clem—"

"He's another sidewinder," growled Ned Gorman.

"Funny thing about *him,*" murmured the taciturn Bill Gorman.

"What do you mean?" Breck eyed the cowman sharply.

"The rustlers don't seem to bother Fish Tay none," explained Bill Gorman. "He's gettin' himself a real nice bunch of cows, for all his shiftless ways."

"Saw some good-looking horses in his corral," Breck said thoughtfully. "Any horse stealing going on?" He looked at Sheriff Sorrel.

The law officer shook his head. "Not round these parts," he answered. "If them horses are stolen stock, they come a long way from here." He shrugged his stooped shoulders. "Wouldn't be surprised none if Fish Tay was mixed up with this rustlin' gang. He's a bad *hombre.*"

"Jim!" Breck's tone was thoughtful. "What became of Tonio?"

"Tonio?" The foreman gave his young boss a surprised look. "You mean that Shoshone half-breed kid that used to keep herd on the milk cows?"

Breck nodded. "Haven't noticed him round since I got back."

"Tonio got married and quit the ranch years ago," Hawker informed him. "Married a Mexican *señorita* and got him a job in Calico. Tends bar at old Jose Moraga's *cantina*." The foreman chuckled. "Tonio did right well for himself. The gal he married was one of Jose's flock of daughters."

"Shore," nodded the sheriff. "I know Tonio. He's smart. He'll own Jose's *cantina* one of these days."

"Get word to him that I want to have a talk with him," Breck instructed the sheriff. "Tonio can be useful to us."

Sheriff Sorrel nodded thoughtfully. "That's a good idee, Breck. Ain't much that goes on in Mexican town that Tonio don't know."

"You figger to use him as a sort o' spy?" Bowie Smith's tone was dubious. "Seems awful risky, Breck. How do you know yuh can trust this Tonio jasper?"

"Tonio would cut his own throat before he'd double-cross Breck," rumbled Jim Hawker. "That Shoshone half-breed figgers Breck next to his God. He owes Breck his life."

"He'll be useful to us," repeated the young Circle B owner. "Shouldn't be surprised if Tonio can tell us a lot about Kirk Bannion."

"I'll round him up for yuh, Breck," promised the sheriff. "It's a right smart idee—"

Footsteps hurried along the hall. Sheriff Sorrel jerked up from his chair.

"Andy Hogan," he muttered. "He's shore in one big rush when he stomps double-time with them high heels—" The old law officer moved quickly to the door and pulled it open.

"Clem!" The bow-legged deputy was breathing hard. "That Ramon feller figgers to talk. He wants you and Breck *pronto*—"

"*Bueno*," muttered the sheriff. He glanced over his shoulder at the others. "That's a break for us, fellers—"

"He's scared to death," Andy told them from the doorway. "He wants to talk, but says yuh've got to git him out of town tonight—or he won't live to see another sunset."

"Let's go!" Breck made for the door.

Jim Hawker glanced at the three cowmen. "Reckon we'll trail along with yuh, Breck—"

They trooped down the hall and down the stairs. At a signal from the Circle B foreman, Johnny Wing and Dusty Rodes followed them into the starlit night.

There was an ominous quiet in the street. The sheriff flung a glance at the brightly lighted entrance of the Outpost Saloon. Four men lounged near the swing doors.

"Al Roan's got us watched," Sorrel muttered to Jim Hawker. "Where've yuh posted them lads of yores, Jim?"

As if in answer to the sheriff's query, two shadowy shapes took form in the doorway of Guttersen's store. The Circle B foreman's gaze raked across the street to the dark murk of the alley between the new brick bank building and Durwan's Saddle & Harness Shop. What he glimpsed there satisfied him.

"No call to worry about Al's Horseshoe gunfighters," he reassured the law officer. "Our boys are on the job. That's Smoky Peters yonder in the alley, an' Larry O'Day an' Slim Lawson is keepin' watch from Guttersen's place." He threw a look at Johnny Wing and Dusty Rodes and melted into the dark toward the alley where Smoky Peters kept vigilant watch. Johnny's stride quickened, carried him past Breck and directly behind the sheriff and Andy Hogan. Dusty's high-heeled boots beat a quick tattoo close on the young cattleman's fast-moving high shape. The latter's grin was affectionate. No matter how deep the morass of grief and treachery, the flame of loyalty to the old Circle B was still burning brightly.

The Calico County bastille was a low, squat building of hand-made adobe bricks and shaded on three sides by thick-branched umbrella trees. Sheriff Sorrel had more than once considered the advisability of cutting the trees down. Their deep, protective shadows were not to the best interests of the jail. His several decisions to stay the ax were to the kindhearted old sheriff's credit. Men confined in that sun-baked jail had reason to be grateful for those cooling, green-leafed branches.

A dim kerosene lamp swung above the entrance. Breck looked over his shoulder. The street behind was in darkness, save for the bright lights of the Outpost Saloon.

"Don't seem natch'ral," muttered Jim Hawker uneasily. "I'm still claimin' you made a fool play —bustin' into this damn cowtown—"

Breck did not hear his foreman's worried voice. He was staring at the man sprawled across the threshold of the open door.

Sheriff Sorrel and Andy Hogan were down on their knees by the side of the limp body. Oaths frothed from the deputy's lips. His chief lifted a hard face to the crowding men.

"He's dead!"

He flung through the door, gun in hand.

Andy Hogan got to his feet. Horror was in the look he flung at the startled faces under the faint yellow glow of the kerosene lantern. His croak was an echo of the sheriff's words.

"He's dead! Knifed in the throat!"

They crowded past the jailer's limp body.

Sheriff Sorrel was bending over another limp form. He looked round as they pounded up the corridor to the iron-barred cell.

"Ramon's dead," he told them curtly. "Looks

like somebody wasn't wantin' Ramon to do any talkin'." The sheriff's gaunt frame lifted and he stared round grimly at the others. "Who do you figger was scared, Breck?"

Breck could only look dazedly at the dead Mexican. No chance, now, for Ramon Matute to tell his story.

"Something queer about this killin'," muttered Jim Hawker. "Whoever done it was no stranger to Ben, nor to Ramon. Ben hadn't drawed his gun. The killer stabbed Ben before he knowed what was happenin'."

They trooped back to the slain jailer. It was plain to their experienced eyes that Hawker was right. Some person well known to the jailer had dealt him the death blow, taken him unaware.

"I wasn't gone more than fifteen minutes," muttered Andy Hogan. "Left Ben sittin' here, making a cigarette. He'd just told me Ramon wanted to talk to you and Breck—"

"Somebody was awful scared," repeated the sheriff. Again he appealed to Breck. "Who do you figger was so scared he would pull off a double killin' inside of fifteen minutes?"

"Anybody been round?" Breck asked the deputy.

"Only Al Roan," answered Andy Hogan. "He wanted to see Ramon. Got awful peeved when I said he couldn't without an order from Clem.

Swore Val Stamper would have Clem's star—"

A tall form loomed out of the darkness.

"What's wrong here?" Kirk Bannion threw a startled look at the dead jailer. "Ben!" he muttered in an aghast voice. "Stabbed to death—" His gaze went to the circle of grim faces. "Who did it, Clem?"

"If we knew who done it, we'd know who knifed Ramon, too," the old sheriff responded dryly.

"Ramon—too!" The lawyer's face paled. "I've come over on purpose to see you about Ramon," he went on. "Val Stamper wanted to bail him out." He shook his head regretfully. "Too bad I wasn't a few minutes sooner, Clem. This wouldn't have happened if we could have bailed that poor Mexican out of here." Bannion looked at Breck suspiciously. "What do you know about this killing, Allen? It was you that had Ramon put into this jail?"

"What are yuh drivin' at, mister?" Old Jim Hawker's voice was tight with anger. "I ain't likin' what yuh say—nor the way yuh say it—"

"Pipe down, Jim," Breck said. "Bannion's not accusing me. Are you, Bannion?" He asked the question softly.

"Somebody killed him—and poor Ben," grumbled the lawyer. "We're going to get to the bottom of this business—why they were killed—and who did the killing."

"You're right, Bannion." Breck's tone was grim. "We're going to get to the bottom of this business—and a lot of other things that need clearing up."

The lawyer swung on his heel. "Val Stamper will want to know about this," he said, with a significant look at Sheriff Sorrel. "Val won't like it, Clem. He's already mighty sore at the way you run your office." He melted into the darkness.

"Trail him," Breck briefly instructed Johnny Wing.

The cowboy vanished up the street, and Breck smiled round grimly at the stern faces of his silent friends.

"You are all witnesses that I was in my room at the hotel when these men were murdered," he said.

"We're with you, son," growled the bearded Bowie Smith.

The Gorman brothers nodded agreement.

"That lawyer-shark figgers to make plenty trouble," muttered the latter. "This Ramon was a low-down coyote, but at that he was on the Horseshoe payroll. Val Stamper'll want yore scalp, Clem—"

"Looks like a showdown for certain," admitted the veteran sheriff mildly. His glance went to Johnny Wing as the latter slid in from the black night. "Well, son—"

"Bannion headed straight for the Outpost," the cowboy informed them.

Jim Hawker looked worriedly at Breck. "You've got to get out of this town, Breck," he urged. "Bannion aims to spill the news. Hell's going to bust loose—"

"Jim's talkin' good horse-sense," agreed the sheriff. His voice was grave. "This Ramon killin' will start off the fireworks—the way things are. There's folks here that want to see you dangling at the end of a rope."

Breck shook his head. He knew these wise old men spoke the truth, yet he could not ride away —*now*—not without Jane Tallant. He could not leave her alone—up there in that big house where she had gone to spend the night with Della Stamper. There was danger for her as well as for him in this town of Calico.

"I'm not running away," he told them quietly. "Let's go back to the hotel. And Jim—send a couple of the boys over to Val Stamper's house. I want the place watched—until Jane gets back to the hotel."

"I'll send Smoky Peters and Larry O'Day," promised the Circle B foreman as he followed into the street.

Chapter Seven

Stalking Shadows

Jane's talk with Della's father was not proving satisfactory, although he listened politely enough to her brief account of the attempts to drive her from Mexican Wells.

"It's an unbelievable story," finally pronounced the banker. "It is not possible that any man in my employ would dare to commit such an outrage, Miss Tallant."

"The horses they rode carried your Horseshoe brand, Mr. Stamper."

"It's an infamous trick, perpetrated by enemies," fumed Della's father. He huddled back in a deep leather chair and stared at her with his cold, unwinking eyes. "An infamous trick," he repeated. "Somebody is using my good name to cloak a monstrous plot against you."

"These men, riding your horses, tried to make me believe they were from the Circle B Ranch," Jane pointed out.

"Mexican Wells is on Circle B range," reminded the old man sourly. "It seems to me, Miss Tallant, that you should turn your suspicions in *that* direction—"

"Such suspicions would be absurd," Jane told

him a bit wearily. "It is true that I was fooled for a time—really believed these threats came from the Circle B people. The fact that my aunt and myself are now guests at the Circle B quite proves that I regard Breck Allen as my friend. I have good reason to trust him."

"And what is this good reason?" queried Val Stamper curiously.

"Breck Allen saved my life. If he had not come to my rescue I would have been murdered in the Painted Canyon."

"How did he know you were in the Painted Canyon?"

"My aunt told him. Breck suspected I was in danger. He had seen these three men riding in that direction. He killed two of them," she finished coolly. "He believes the Mexican that Sheriff Sorrel arrested is the third of the trio—the man who escaped on a bald-faced horse."

The banker was silent for a long minute. Jane sensed that her account of the fight was news to him.

"I assure you that I don't know a thing about this affair," he finally said. "I have sent no orders to my foreman, Al Roan, to frighten you away from your Mexican Wells homestead, and I certainly have not plotted your murder. It is absurd to in any way connect me with these crimes."

"I haven't really thought you were, Mr. Stamper," Jane admitted honestly. "I've told

Breck Allen that it was too utterly absurd to suspect that you were behind this lawless business. The wretched angle is the fact that these men seem to be from your ranch. They ride your horses."

"I don't understand it," frowned the banker. "I'm as much mystified as you are."

"This Ramon Matute *is* one of your riders," Jane reminded. "I heard your lawyer, Mr. Bannion, admit it to Breck over at the hotel."

"It's a complete mystery," muttered Val Stamper. He gave the girl a strange look. "Has it occurred to you that these attacks on you began before Breck Allen's recent return? How do you know that they were not instigated by his father? Young Breck would possibly know nothing of the affair for the reason that his father was—well, apparently murdered a few days before Breck reached home."

Jane shook her head. "I cannot conceive of such a possibility," she demurred stoutly. She went on thoughtfully. "Of course I know of the feud between the two ranches—and that you've always hated Breck's father—and Breck—"

"Breck shot my son—my only son." The words came in a croak from the old man's bloodless lips. "That young man is a killer at heart. You have just admitted he killed two men the day of his return to the Calico country—"

"He was defending me—"

"Breck Allen murdered my boy," gasped the owner of the Horseshoe Ranch.

"It's a lie!"

Della Stamper stood in the doorway, indignation flaming in the look she flung at her father.

"It's about time you let up on Breck," she flared. "All the decent people in this country believe him innocent. Clem Sorrel has talked to me about it. Clem says that Breck can prove his innocence if he has a chance!"

"Leave the room, child," said the old man harshly. "You were too young to know anything about it."

"I won't leave the room!" stormed the red-headed girl. "I wasn't too young! I was thirteen—and Breck was always so nice to me. I can never believe he killed Tom—"

Her father eyed her sharply. "You've seen Breck—today?"

"Yes, I have!" Della's quick smile was self-conscious. "He's adorable, daddy. I want you to patch up this silly old quarrel with the Circle B. I want Breck for a friend." She paused, colored under Jane's shrewd look. "Breck is the first man I've met since I've grown up that I could really like a lot—"

"You're a silly young girl," grumbled Val Stamper. "Leave the room immediately. I'll attend to you later, missie."

Della tossed her bright head, made a face at

him. "Daddy just won't believe I'm grown up," she complained to Jane.

"Leave the room," repeated her father crossly. "Miss Tallant and I have private matters—"

"I want to talk to Jane," pouted his daughter. "She's my guest—"

"I'll be with you in a few minutes," promised Jane.

Della withdrew reluctantly. Her father gave Jane a rueful smile.

"Della's spoiled," he grumbled. "She likes to have what she wants."

"Perhaps she takes after her father," Jane told him a bit wickedly. "I understand that you usually get what you want, too, Mr. Stamper."

The banker waved a complacent hand. "I'm not often disappointed," he admitted dryly.

"Except when you have wanted something the Allens won't let you take," countered the girl. She watched him under lowered lashes. "Why do you want Mexican Wells, Mr. Stamper? Why do you want the Circle B Cactus Hills range?"

A curious light gleamed in the murky depths of his eyes.

"I'll ask *you* a question, Miss Tallant. Why do *you* want Mexican Wells? What is *your* interest in the Painted Canyon?"

"Perhaps I want to go into the cattle business," parried the girl. "It would be exciting to be a cattle queen—"

"Nonsense!" he scoffed. "Not in that desert!"

"—or perhaps I'm interested in geology," Jane went on, giving him a wide-eyed innocent smile. "The rock formation is most interesting up in the Painted Canyon—"

"You mean you're prospecting?" interrupted Stamper quickly. He cackled. "You're wasting your time, young woman—if you expect to find gold in those hills."

"Gold is where you find it, mister," laughed Jane. She continued to eye him slyly under curling long lashes.

The banker glowered at her, made a sudden gesture and reached a checkbook from a drawer in his desk.

"Your observation is sometimes more true than is usually the case," he told her a trifle grimly. "I feel sorry for you, young woman. Whatever fool's errand brought you to Mexican Wells has surely been paid for in bitter experience. You and your aunt have suffered. I'm disposed to help you to the extent of five thousand dollars, if you agree to leave this country and go back to where you came from."

Jane stifled a gasp, and then she said coolly, "You offered Breck's father *ten* thousand to vacate the Cactus Hills country, Mr. Stamper. I'm afraid you are not quite fair—"

The old cattleman glared at her fixedly.

"You seem to know a lot," he grunted.

"Not as much as I want to know," she confessed with a shrug of slim shoulder. "I was hoping you could tell me a few things—for instance, why you are so anxious to possess Mexican Wells and the adjacent Cactus Hills—"

He sat huddled back in the great leather chair, cold unwinking eyes probing her. Jane was aware of a sudden repulsion for the vulture-like head poking toward her. Was this dreadful old man aware of her identity? she wondered. Was it possible he knew the story of her missing father? He had at no time intimated that her name was familiar. She thought of the scrap of paper tucked inside her cowboy flannel shirt.

"You have an odd name for your ranch," she said suddenly. "How did you come to call your cattle ranch the Horseshoe, Mr. Stamper?"

"My brand is in the shape of a horseshoe," he explained. "What is there odd about a horse-shoe, Miss Tallant?" His tone was frankly suspicious.

"You must have had some reason," persisted the girl. She hesitated, struggling with the temptation to ask if he had ever heard of the lost Horseshoe Lode. "I was just wondering," she finished lamely.

"There's a saying that a horseshoe brings luck," Val Stamper reminded. His smile sent a shiver through the girl.

She rose. "I'll run along to Della now," she

said. "It was sweet of her to ask me to spend the night—"

He motioned for her to sit down. "You haven't answered my questions—explained your interest in Mexican Wells and the Painted Canyon—" Jane guessed shrewdly that he was forcing himself to be pleasant. "Perhaps we can be of use to each other, Miss Tallant."

"I see no reason why I should answer your questions," Jane told him bluntly. "You do not care to answer mine." She moved toward the door, vaguely aware of hurrying feet. "At least Breck Allen may learn something from Ramon Matute—when he talks. Breck says the man will talk to save his own skin."

The door flung open. The newcomer was Kirk Bannion. For a moment he failed to see the girl, partially concealed behind the open door. He spoke excitedly to the old man huddled in the big chair.

"The Mexican's dead," he said. "Somebody got into the jail and knifed him—and the jailer." The lawyer broke off, turned a startled look on Jane. "I didn't see you," he apologized politely.

She was staring at him with horrified eyes. "You mean Ramon is dead—murdered?" she stammered.

Bannion bowed. "Yes," he told her smoothly. "The killing has caused a lot of excitement down the street. There's talk that Breck Allen framed the killing to close the Mexican's mouth—"

"It's a dreadful lie!" Jane cried furiously. She ran from the room.

Della intercepted her in the hall. The young girl's face was pale.

"Jane! What's wrong? I heard Kirk Bannion say something about Breck!"

Jane repeated the lawyer's brief words. Her lips were stiff with fear. The red-headed girl's eyes widened with horror and quick indignation.

"It can't be true!" she wailed. "It's a miserable plot to make trouble for poor Breck. Oh, Jane—it makes me sick!" She flew down the hall and vanished into her father's library.

Jane made her way up the stairs to her room. The shades were up, letting in the soft moonlight. She went to the window, conscious of a growing dismay that bordered on panic. There could be no thought of bed now. She wanted to get away from this house. She wanted to be with Breck Allen—wanted to warn him of his danger.

Frightened and miserable, the girl stared into the moonlit night. She could see the faint glow of the kerosene street lamps below the hill.

Her door flew open and Della rushed into the room.

"Jane!" The girl's voice trembled. "It's too dreadful! Kirk Bannion says there's talk of lynching Breck!"

The red-headed Della's hysteria had a stiffening effect on Jane. She eyed the girl coolly.

"What does your father say? Can't he do something—"

"Kirk says it's useless to interfere." Della was trying not to weep. "He—he says there'll be bloodshed—if the sheriff tries to stop them."

"But what does your father say?" repeated Jane impatiently. "He's the big man in this town, I'm told—"

"Dad agrees with Kirk. He's terribly upset, but he won't do anything." Della slumped down on the bed and stared tearfully at the other girl. "I can't stand it, Jane. Johnny Wing will be dragged into it . . . he'll be killed . . . trying to—to help Breck—"

Jane sat down by her side, tried to comfort her. She quite understood Della's terror. She felt the same way about Breck.

"You like Johnny?"

Della nodded. "He doesn't know, but I'm crazy about him. I guess he thinks I'm an awful little flirt, but I'll just die—if anything happens to Johnny."

"You go and talk some more to your father," counseled Jane. She pushed the girl to the door. "Make him do something—"

She locked the door and hurried back to the window. She was going to Breck . . . his life depended on being warned in time. She feared to leave by the front door. Her talk with Val Stamper had increased her distrust of the man.

He might stop her. Jane was skeptical of his wish to save Breck from mob violence. Val Stamper wanted Breck lynched, if for no other reason than that he regarded Breck as the slayer of his son. It would not be safe to attempt to leave the house by way of the front door, Jane reasoned. She could not afford the risk of being detained by force. Perhaps she was doing Val Stamper an injustice—but there was too much at stake to give him a chance to keep her from warning Breck.

The wide window was already open. Jane stepped out to the narrow balcony. She could not jump down, but she could slide down one of the slender round columns that supported the balcony.

Cautiously she climbed over the balcony rail and hung her full length, feeling for the column. Her legs clamped over the smooth round pillar. She let herself go, grateful for the protective boots under her overalls. It was a breath-taking slide. In a moment her feet were on firm ground, and after a moment's pause to quiet the beating of her heart, she stole cautiously through the shrubbery.

A shape suddenly moved in the moonlight.

Jane froze against a bush. Another shape appeared, joined the first man. The girl cowered in an agony of apprehension. The two men had seen her—were slowly approaching. Moonshine glinted on their drawn guns.

Chapter Eight

Dangerous Night

Jane's heart stood still. Escape was impossible now, unless she could bluff her way past those stalking shapes that were men. Desperately she fought off her panic and sauntered into the moonlit path. There was a chance they had not seen her climb down from the balcony. If questioned she could say she was Della's guest, enjoying a bedtime stroll in the garden.

The men halted. Jane continued her slow saunter toward them, pretending not to notice their shadowy forms under the dense gloom of a locust tree. She forced herself to be ready with a friendly, casual smile.

One of the high shapes stirred under the shadowy branches, moved to intercept her.

"Miss Jane—" The man's face bent close to her for a moment, swung a look round at his motionless companion. "It's Miss Jane, Larry."

The girl's heart began to race. "Smoky Peters!" Relief poured through her. She wanted to shout the cowboy's name.

"No noise," he muttered. "Coupla fellers watchin' at the front door—"

"Who sent you, Smoky?" Jane asked in a whisper.

"The boss wasn't easy about yuh, Miss Jane," the cowboy briefly explained. "Figgered you wasn't safe here—"

His companion disentangled himself from the shadows and Jane recognized Larry O'Day. He whispered for a moment with Smoky, then disappeared with Indian stealth into the shrubbery. Smoky grinned reassuringly at the girl.

"We figgered it was you climbin' down from the window," he chuckled. "Shore spunky of yuh, Miss Jane—"

"I had to get away," Jane told him. "Breck's in great danger. He must be warned."

Smoky beckoned her into the deeper shadows. "There's a couple of fellers watching at the front door," he repeated.

"Bannion's in the house," whispered the girl. "I heard him tell Val Stamper that they're planning to lynch Breck—because of that Mexican—"

The cowboy nodded grimly. "Al Roan's in there, too," he said. "Followed Bannion a couple of minutes ago and left those two jaspers on watch."

"Oh, Smoky,"—Jane's voice quavered—"we've got to get away from here! Breck must be warned."

"You wait here," ordered the cowboy. "Don't yuh move away. We've got to fix them two *hombres*—" He slid into the bushes.

Jane found herself unable to obey Smoky's

command to wait. She followed his vague shape through the moondrift. Larry O'Day's face peered round at them from a clump of young tamarisks.

"I've got this thing figgered out, Smoky," he muttered. "You stay back with the gal." He moved forward, bent low behind the tamarisk hedge.

There was a minute's breathless suspense. Suddenly they saw Larry gliding through the moonlight toward the two unsuspecting men lounging near the front steps.

"He's got 'em," murmured Smoky. "Make dust for the gate, Miss Jane. We'll be with yuh in a jiffy." He hurried to help his companion disarm the two surprised Horseshoe men.

Jane sped to the gate, careful to hug the shadows. Smoky and Larry overtook her with the sullen-faced prisoners.

"Reckon we'll tie these birds up," Smoky decided.

"Better fix 'em so they won't do some loud yellin'," suggested his companion.

Jane waited in a fever of impatience while the Circle B men securely trussed and gagged the captured look-outs and dragged them to a brush-grown gully below the fence.

"What'll we do with the broncs?" queried Larry with a gesture at the horses tied to the hitch-rail in front of the garden gate.

"No time to monkey with 'em," Smoky said. "No sense givin' 'em a chance to call us horse thieves. Come on, Miss Jane, we can make the hotel in less than ten minutes."

She raced along at his noiseless heels, Larry trailing behind. Smoky threw an encouraging grin over his shoulder.

"We'll cut into the alley," he told her. "Jim has one of the boys posted at the back door—"

Soon they were down the slope and moving swiftly up the dusty alley to the rear of the Haley House. A man suddenly loomed out of the shadows. Smoky halted.

"That you, Cheyenne?"

The man lowered his gun. "Smoky!" Surprise looked from Cheyenne's eyes as he peered at Jane. "What yuh want, feller?"

"We want in," grunted the cowboy. "You know Miss Jane. She's got news for the boss—" He pushed through the door. Jane followed him into the kitchen where a fat Chinese cook was busy with pots and pans. Smoky gave him a friendly grin.

"Hi, Wong! Shore was good pie we had for supper."

The fat cook beamed at him, gave the girl a brief look from incurious eyes.

"Where's the back stairs, Wong?" asked Smoky. "The young lady don't want to be seen out front."

The cook's gesture indicated a small door.

The cowboy jerked it open and led the way up the dark stair. Larry O'Day pulled the door shut and followed behind. Jane's heart warmed to these quick-thinking cowboys who served Breck Allen so loyally.

A ribbon of light showed under the door; they heard the rumble of voices that hushed at the sound of their hurrying feet. Smoky grinned at the girl.

"Jim Hawker's with him. That was Jim's voice." He rapped softly. "Jim—it's me—"

The door opened. Heedless of the surprised faces, Jane ran to Breck. He sprang to his feet.

"Breck!" She seized his hand. "You must get away from this town before it's too late—"

"I thought you went to Della's for the night," he broke in.

"I've just come from there. I climbed out of the window. I had to see you Breck—warn you! Oh, please, let's get out of this town—"

An uproar suddenly broke the stillness of the outside night, a wave of berserk sound that left Jane trembling.

"They—they're coming to lynch you," she gasped. "Breck—I heard Kirk Bannion tell Mr. Stamper—"

"She's got it right," muttered Smoky Peters. "We got her away from there, boss, after she climbed out of the window. Had to hog-tie a couple of Al Roan's gun-slingers—"

Shouts and curses floated up from the street. Sheriff Sorrel got to his feet. His lined face was drawn with worry. "I'll go down an' talk to 'em," he said quietly. He gave Jim Hawker a grim look. "Git yore boys together, Jim. We've got to keep that mob out of this hotel." His tall shape slid into the hall.

The Circle B foreman gave Smoky and Larry a look that sent them hurrying after the sheriff. "Tell Johnny an' Dusty I want 'em up here," he called after them.

Bowie Smith and his two fellow ranchers eyed each other worriedly.

"You men get out of this," Breck told them.

The bearded Lazy S man shook his head. "We're standin' by you, Breck," he answered simply.

Ned and Bill Gorman nodded agreement. Jane looked pleadingly at Jim Hawker.

"Can't you do something—get him away? They'll murder him—"

"I'm not running away," Breck said quietly. "I'm not afraid of these men. I'll talk to them—" He moved toward the door, suddenly found the girl clinging to him.

"I'm frightened," she moaned. "I—I want to get away! Take me away, Breck—"

There was something bestial in that low growl of the mob that had suddenly filled the street. A gun crashed. Jane clung tightly to Breck. Again her eyes sought old Jim Hawker. He read her purpose. Breck would not leave to save himself. It was not in him to run away from personal danger. He must be made to believe that it was for the sake of Jane's life he must consent to leave town.

"She's right, Breck," the Circle B foreman urged his young boss. "You've got to get her away from this place."

"Please," reiterated the girl hysterically. "I'm frightened. You know how those men tried to kill me in Painted Canyon!" Her arms tightened round him.

"All right, Jane," he soothed gently. "We'll get you away—" He felt her weight go limp against him.

Mat Haley hurried into the room. The hotel man's face was haggard.

"They got Clem Sorrel," he told them agitatedly. "Got him hog-tied—an' wounded Andy Hogan."

A fusillade of shots crashed in the street.

"I got all the doors barred," Mat Haley went on. "They won't get in easy—not with yore boys waitin' inside ready to fill 'em with lead."

"You can go down the back stairs," Jim Hawker suggested, looking at Breck.

The latter shook his head dubiously. "They'll be watching the back door. No chance that way, Jim—"

"There's the roof," broke in Mat Haley. "It's

flat—and I've a ladder that'll reach across to Guttersen's roof. You can climb down his fire escape."

"We'll try it," Breck said briefly. He felt Jane's slim body straighten up. She looked slyly round at Jim Hawker, gave him a faint smile. "Can you make it?" Breck asked her.

"If I can slide down a balcony post, I should be able to manage a fire escape," retorted Jane.

"Let's go," Breck said curtly.

The grumbling of the mob swelled to thunder. Jane thought she had never heard such fiendish yells. Gunfire in the street rattled the windows, and from below stairs came the crackle of .45's.

"Johnny and Dusty will get yore horses from the barn," Jim Hawker told Breck. "No sense for you and Jane to go to the barn. Better make for that coulee below Spanish Town and wait there for the broncs."

The foreman's plan was sound, Breck realized.

"All right," he agreed. "Show us up to the roof, Mat."

They hurried into the hall to a narrow stairway. Johnny and Dusty went up, followed by Breck and Jane.

"The ladder's lyin' near the rear parapet," Mat Haley called to them. He hastened to overtake Jim Hawker and the three cowmen, clattering down the stairs to join the defenders below.

"This moonlight ain't so good," muttered

Johnny Wing as he and Dusty Rodes pushed the ladder across space to Guttersen's adjoining roof. "Be too bad if they spot us crawlin' over this ladder."

Another burst of gunfire rose above the howls of the mob in the street.

"The boys are keepin' the coyotes busy," Dusty Rodes chuckled. He peered over the three foot parapet. "Alley's all clear," he announced. "Who's goin' over first?"

"Reckon I'll try her out first," Johnny said. "Got to have somebody at the other end to hold her steady for Miss Jane."

"I'm first over, Johnny," grinned Breck. "You keep your eyes peeled for trouble below."

"I'm watchin'," grunted the cowboy. He peered into the alley, six-gun in hand.

"You follow me," Breck told Jane. "All right, Dusty, hang onto the ladder—"

"I'd rather be a cat right now," muttered Dusty. "Never was no'count walkin' a tight-rope—"

Jane eyed the flimsy, improvised bridge doubtfully. It was a full fifteen feet to the opposite roof, and twenty-five feet to the ground below.

"I'm not sure, Breck—" Her tone was dubious. "I'm like Dusty—when it comes to walking a tight-rope—"

"All right, Dusty—you're elected to play first cat." Breck grinned, bent down to hold the ladder. "Watch that street, Johnny," he warned.

Dusty stepped gingerly to the stout, wide rungs and went across with painful slowness. In another moment he was down on the roof and steadying his end of the ladder.

"All clear below," Johnny announced. He took Breck's place at the ladder. "I'll hold her for yuh—"

Breck turned to Jane and picked her up in his arms.

"You—you can't!" she gasped.

He was already stepping up to the ladder. Jane closed her eyes, lay breathless in the strong arms that held her so easily. There was something reassuring in the even beat of his heart. She heard Johnny Wing's voice, low and tense.

"Steady, boss—"

The gun in his hand crackled twice. Breck's smooth stride across the rungs of the ladder continued without a falter. She felt his feet come firmly to rest on Guttersen's roof, but still her arms clung round his neck. She felt oddly trembly now that it was over. Death had been very close, she knew.

"It's all right, Jane." Breck's voice was husky. Jane felt a sudden hammering of the heart that had been so steady during those seconds of peril. Her eyes opened and for a moment Breck looked into their blue-black depths. She smiled tremulously, slid from his embrace and turned to watch Johnny Wing make his precarious passage over that frail and narrow bridge. He sprang from the coping and craned his head for a look into the alley below.

Jane peered down, saw the limp body sprawled in the dust. She shuddered.

"Got the *hombre* before he could pull trigger," muttered Johnny. His blue eyes were like ice. "Hell's too good for *his* sort—tryin' to potshot you when you was carryin' *her*—" The cowboy's voice was unsteady, and with a shame-faced grin he hurried to join Dusty at the fire escape.

Sporadic bursts of gunfire continued to assail the night as they fled across the roof. Fierce yells and curses mingled with the roar of six-guns. Jane found herself clinging to Breck's hand.

The fire escape was easy after the perils of the ladder. They swung down and raced across the littered yard to the board fence. The gate was padlocked. Dusty scrambled to the top of the five foot barricade and reached for the girl. She swung up to his side, boosted by Breck.

Booted feet clattered noisily in the store, the back door banged open. Breck and Johnny Wing whirled, guns spouting red fire at the little group of men charging toward them. Dusty, straddled over the board fence, gave Jane a push that sent her in a wild leap to the other side. His own .45 began to crackle.

The girl stood where she had landed, frozen with fear, her ears shocked with the groans of dying men, the horrid sound of their choked retching. Breck's face suddenly appeared from behind the lifting smoke, and at his back, the grim hard faces of Johnny and Dusty. Their booted feet thudded to the ground and again they were racing into the night.

From somewhere a rifle flashed at them. Jane heard the sinister hum of a bullet. They dived into a clump of mesquite and scrambled down the steep side of an arroyo. The girl's breath was coming in gasps. Again the rifle flashed, this time from the bank above them. Johnny's gun sent back an answering bullet and something heavy went toppling down the steep side of the arroyo.

"Got him!" grunted the Circle B's premier marksman. "That makes four of 'em won't follow our trail no more, Dusty."

They went pounding down the bed of the arroyo, Jane gamely keeping the pace by Breck's side.

"How much further?" she gasped.

He sensed her weariness and reached for her hand.

"Not far," he encouraged. "Just round the bend."

Another hundred yards brought them to a bit of marshy ground thickly overgrown with willow and cottonwood trees. Jane sank down on a boulder.

"I couldn't run one more yard," she declared between gasps.

"Ma'am," admired Johnny Wing. "Yuh've shore got the speed an' wind of a jackrabbit."

"Hope they didn't hear our gunplay," worried Dusty Rodes. "They'll be hot on our trail if they heard the shootin'—"

Breck thought not. The shooting was so general down in the street, he doubted that the mob's attention would be drawn to the scene of the fight in Guttersen's yard.

Johnny agreed. "It's the broncs that'll be a tough job," he worried in turn. "That bunch'll be watchin' Horner's place."

Again Breck thought not.

"They're too busy up at the hotel," he pointed out. "They think I'm still there. They'll figure they've got the whole Circle B outfit penned up in the Haley House."

"Got yore wind back, feller?" Johnny grinned at his range mate. "Let's get goin' for them horses."

Dusty announced he was ready to sprint another ten miles. Breck eyed the girl questioningly.

"How about you, Jane?"

"I'm ready to outrun Dusty this very minute," she declared spiritedly.

"Jim said you was to stay here," demurred Johnny. "No sense you goin' to the barn, boss. We'll snake them broncs out of there."

"Reckon we'll trail along with you," smiled the young cattleman. "There's a back door to that barn, and Jim said he would leave a couple of our boys inside to keep watch."

The two cowboys exchanged dubious looks.

"No tellin' what we'll run into, boss," began Johnny.

Breck ignored his protests.

"We're wasting time," he said curtly. "Let's go."

They pushed through the willows and cut into a trail that wound up the arroyo slope and presently found themselves on the outskirts of the town, with the big livery barn looming between them and the beleaguered hotel. Breck halted.

"Time for some scout work," he said laconically.

Johnny and Dusty slid like Indians through the thick mesquite. Jane saw the longing look in Breck's eyes.

"You want to go, too," she said. "I'm an awful nuisance, Breck."

He hesitated, shook his head.

"I'm not letting you out of my sight again, Jane. I shouldn't have allowed you to go with Della to that house."

"It's turned out for the best that I *did* go," Jane retorted. "You—you wouldn't have known in time to—to—" She found herself crying softly against his shoulder.

"Jane—Jane!" Remorse was in his voice. "I didn't mean—"

She smiled up at him through her tears.

"I'm silly . . . just nerves—"

There was a rustle in the underbrush. Dusty Rodes glided up.

"Looks pretty good," he told them cheerfully. "Barn doors closed in front, with one of Al Roan's gun-slingers on watch outside. Reckon Johnny'll have the jasper hog-tied, time we get to the back door."

They drifted quietly through the moon-silvered chaparral.

Johnny Wing took shape by the side of the long livery barn. His contented grin told them that he had successfully attended to Al Roan's guard.

"Turned him over to Shorty an' Hank," he chuckled. "Had to tap him real hard on his fool head. He's sleepin' it off in the hayloft, an' tied up all nice with baling wire."

Shorty and Hank were watching for them. The big door in the rear of the barn swung open, revealed the gray stallion and Jane's brown mare.

Shorty led the animals out, and Breck and Jane climbed into their saddles.

"You can turn your prisoner loose in half an hour or so," Breck told Johnny. "He'll spread the news down the street."

"I savvy," nodded the cowboy. "The mob'll quit

hellin' round the hotel when the news spreads, yuh're gone. Jim and the rest of us will be right on yore tail inside of an hour, boss."

"*Aidios*, boys. See you at the ranch—"

Gray horse and brown mare melted into the moonlit landscape.

Breck eyed down at the brown mare's slim rider. She met his look with a smile that closed his ears to the sounds of berserk fury behind him.

He rode on, aware of an oddly pleasing sensation. The trail that wound through mesquite and bristling cactus was suddenly a smooth, broad highway that reached on and on through a fair country.

Perhaps Jane sensed his thoughts. There was a starry look in her eyes as she rode by his side, a singing in her heart.

<u>Chapter Nine</u>

Ambush

Breck gloomily eyed the big, dog-eared ledger spread open on the battered, flat-topped desk. There was no disputing the facts he had finally worried from that musty old tome. The Circle B was badly in the red. The once prosperous ranch was faced with bankruptcy.

He leaned back in the creaky swivel chair and thoughtfully made a cigarette, gaze idling around the roomy office. In earlier days this low adobe had been the ranch-house. It was not until Breck's father had brought his young bride from her Virginia home that the present rambling and comfortable house had been built. Since then, the old adobe had served as the ranch office. It stood some hundred feet back from the patio garden, with a window that gave a view on the corrals, its gray walls and red-tiled roof shaded by hoary cottonwood trees.

There was a wide fireplace in one end of the room, with a pair of tremendous horns over the mantel. Saddles and bridles and all the paraphernalia of a big cattle ranch adorned the walls and filled the adjoining room. A gun-rack stood near Breck's elbow and above the old desk hung an ancient Sharps buffalo gun. His father's!

Old Breck Allen had been a mighty hunter in the days when the West was young. Buffalo hunter, fur trader, scout and Indian fighter, always a frontiersman—one of the last of a virile breed of empire builders.

There was a cold light in Breck's gray eyes as his gaze went back to the grimy old ledger half buried under a litter of tally sheets. Somewhere in the Calico country lived a man—the man who had slain his father. For Breck there would never be peace of mind until the assassin had been brought to justice.

The thud of hoofs jerked him out of his dark reverie. Jim Hawker swung down from a black-maned buckskin and came with stiff short stride into the office. There was a worried look on the old foreman's weather-bitten face. He pulled a chair close to the desk and sank down with a grunt. Dust clung to his bushy brows and long mustaches.

"Goin' over the papers, huh?" He glanced briefly at the littered desk.

"Things look tough, Jim." The young ranch-man's smile was mirthless. "Looks like our cows don't go in for motherhood any more."

The grizzled foreman nodded gloomily. "Mebbe I'm too old for my job, Breck. Seems like I've been in the cattle business long enough to keep rustlers off this range." He wiped his hot dusty face with a red bandana. "Good thing you're back, son. Mebbe yuh can put the old Circle B on her feet ag'in."

"We can do nothing until we find the answer to a question that's bothering a lot of us cattlemen," Breck said.

"Who's the boss of these damn rustlers," Jim Hawker growled. "Yuh mean we've got to dig this wolf out of his hole, huh?"

Breck nodded. "Jim," he went on, "it's in my mind that my father had learned the man's name —which was why he was murdered."

"I guess yuh're right, son," muttered the old foreman. "He was killed because he knew who was back of this cow-stealin'."

"He's clever," Breck mused. "He's no ordinary cow-thief, Jim."

"Val Stamper ain't no fool when it comes to plenty brains." Hawker's tone was grim. "Have yuh dropped him from yore list, Breck?"

"I have no list of suspects yet." The young boss of the Circle B stared out of the window reflectively. A bawling trail herd was pouring into the big main corral. "How did the roundup turn out, Jim?"

The foreman scowled. "Plenty bad," he grumbled. "Combed ev'ry canyon an' gully in twenty miles for that bunch the boys is pushin' in."

"How many beef steers—ready for the drive?"

"Nine hundred, I figger," Hawker told him gloomily. "Some of 'em poor stuff."

Breck's face was expressionless. He knew the thoughts that tortured the faithful heart of this old retainer. The days had been when never less than a thousand prime beef steers would be gathered for the long drive to railhead.

Dust lifted a dun pall above the corrals, shrill yips of urging cowboys mingled with the resentful bawls of the weary cattle.

"We got to do something, Breck! And damn quick—or we're all washed up with the cattle business!" Hawker swore feelingly. "We got to fix these rustlers—"

"It's a mystery what they do with our cows," Breck said. "Where do they go—after they steal 'em?"

The foreman shook his grizzled head despondently. He was a tired and discouraged old man, Breck realized. Jim had been with the Circle B since his youth. He was all of seventy now—and worn with years and worry.

Compassion and affection were in the look Breck gave him.

"No use to fret, Jim," he said gently. "We're not licked by a long shot."

The foreman's face brightened. "That's man talk," he grinned. "Son, I've set more than one onery cow-thief dancin' on air in my time—me

122

an' yore dad." His big-knuckled hand clenched. "Me an' you will see some more of 'em swingin' from the end of a rope, I reckon."

"I reckon we will," agreed Breck soberly. He glanced through the window. "When do you start the drive, Jim?"

"Aim to let 'em rest up overnight," Hawker told him. "I figger sun-up will see 'em movin'—"

"Going through Shoshone Pass?"

Hawker nodded. "Some longer—but better feed, and cuts out fordin' the river. Lot of quicksand there."

"You're taking a chance," frowned Breck. "Shoshone Pass is too close to the Pot Holes. Almost impossible to gather the herd if the rustlers get to you—stampede you—"

"I figger we can take care of this small bunch," declared Hawker. He lifted out of the chair and turned to the door. "Bowie Smith sent word he'd be over tonight," he added. "He's bringin' Ned Gorman and Bill—and a couple of other fellers. Bowie says it's time we got busy an' organized this vigilante thing."

"I'm not going to be rushed," Breck said curtly. "I'm going to work this out my own way."

"Mebbe yuh're right, son," agreed the old man. "The feller back of this rustlin' has brains—an' it's brains—an' only brains that can lick him. You've got brains, son. I don't blame you for wantin' to play a lone hand." He grinned cheer-fully and stepped up to his saddle.

Breck watched the buckskin mince off toward the corrals. Jim was too old for the rigors of a trail drive, he reflected. It was not fair to leave the responsibility for the safe delivery of that small yet precious herd to Jim. It would take diplomacy—to arrange for himself to go in the old foreman's place.

A shadow fell across the open doorway. Breck swung round from his frowning contemplation of the ledger.

"Hi, mister!" Jane smiled at him. "I was under the impression that we were riding this afternoon at four o'clock. You promised to show me the evening shadows creep across the desert."

She was in overalls and chaps, a white Stetson rakishly set on her dark curls. There was approval in Breck's eyes as he rose from the creaky chair.

"I've been awfully busy—"

"Oh, if you are *too* busy, I could ride by myself to the buttes—only I've sort of promised Aunt Sally not to ride out alone." Jane made a grimace. "Auntie is not the same since our little adventure up in Painted Canyon—quite lost her well-known courage—"

"Indeed I have not," indignantly interrupted a voice. Aunt Sally peered into the office. "Don't you believe the impudent girl, Breck." Her shrewd, bright eyes twinkled behind the steel-rimmed spectacles. "You know me, Breck. I'm the only woman who ever took your guns away from you at the point of a gun." She chuckled.

"I'll never hear the last of it." Breck put on a woebegone look and reached for hat and gun-holster.

Aunt Sally's face sobered. "Seriously, Breck," she went on, "after the dreadful things that have happened, it is not safe for Jane to ride out on the range alone. You can't deny that you both have dangerous enemies."

"If I ever catch her riding off by her lone-some, I'll put hobbles on the girl," Breck promised solemnly.

"Yes, you will *not!*" jeered Aunt Sally's niece.

Aunt Sally beamed approval. "You heard him, Jane," she said severely. "Breck will do it, too, so you mind what we say." She peered interestedly into the office. "What a delightful old place! So smelly of leather and guns and tobacco smoke. A real he-man place." Aunt Sally chuckled and went on her way.

"I wasn't forgetting you," Breck assured Jane. "It's exactly four o'clock—and here comes Manuel with the horses." He added a bit reproachfully, "I hope I'll never be too busy for a ride with *you,* Jane."

The girl's color heightened. "You compli-ment me, Mister Allen," she murmured. Her eyes laughed at him.

They rode across the yard to the corrals, where Johnny Wing and Dusty Rodes hailed them from the top of the split-rail fence.

"Hi, Miss Jane!"

"Hi, Johnny . . . hi, Dusty!" The girl gave the begrimed, grinning cowboys a warm smile. There was a hearty friendship between them since that unforgettable night in Calico. "Where are Smoky and Larry?" she wanted to know.

"Ma'am, them worthless, no 'count punchers ain't worth yore worry," derided Johnny Wing. "They'd be all swelled up if they knowed you was askin' 'bout their health."

"Johnny an' me'll be gettin' jealous of them two bronc peelers," grinned Dusty.

"Why—you terrible boys!" cried Jane indignantly. "Smoky Peters and Larry O'Day are a pair of darlings!"

Johnny Wing threw up his hands in mock despair and promptly tumbled from his perch backwards into the corral. Jane's amused laugh choked to a startled squeal as a wild-eyed steer charged with lowered horns at the luckless cowboy.

Shouts warned Johnny of his impending doom. With a horrified glance at the steer he completed a double backward leap that landed him inside a horse chute.

The laughter returned to the girl's lips.

"See what you get, for saying mean things

about Smoky and Larry," she cried. "Oh, Johnny
—you looked just too funny."

She spurred to overtake Breck.

"You've got those cowboys daffy about you,"
he chuckled.

"Johnny Wing's nice," she declared. "I like
him." Jane laughed. "I've found out something
about him. What do you think, Breck? That poor
kid is in love with Della Stamper."

Breck frowned. "That red-headed girl's a heart-
breaker."

"I could tell you something else about her,"
murmured Jane with a demure smile.

"Not interested," grinned Breck.

Jane threw him a mischievous glance. "Mr.
Stamper told me that Della likes to get what she
wants. She's a chip off the old block."

"Are you warning me?" Breck frowned. "Della
needs a spanking," he grumbled.

They splashed across the shallows of a creek
and cut into a trail that followed the twisting
ascent of a canyon. The murmur of the stream
was presently lost in the depths, and suddenly
they were over the ridge, the vast sweep of the
desert spread below.

Jane's gaze fastened on towering Telescope
Peak. Death Valley lay over there. Her eyes
darkened.

"I'm wasting time," she complained. "I should
be going about my business, Breck."

He knew she referred to her father.

"I won't feel satisfied until I know what has happened to him." Jane's voice trembled. "I—I have the feeling they were both murdered, Breck —and that the Painted Canyon holds the secret."

Breck stared thoughtfully across the floor of the desert now softened with the lavender and pink of approaching sunset. A week had passed since the night he had fled for his life with Jane from Calico. The mob had broken up upon learning of his escape, and Jim Hawker and the sheriff had later convinced Kirk Bannion and Val Stamper that Breck was in their company at the time of the Mexican's murder.

Val Stamper had apparently abandoned his resolve to further prosecute his charge against the young Circle B man for the killing of his son, according to Clem Sorrel's story. Breck had made no further attempt to see the banker. In fact Val Stamper was not in town, the sheriff sent word. He had disappeared the morning following the attempt to lynch Breck, and his whereabouts was something of a mystery. Della professed ignorance, save that her father might have gone to his ranch. This was not the case, wrote the sheriff, who had journeyed out to the Horseshoe to see Al Roan about the slain Mexican. Val Stamper had not been seen at the ranch, Al Roan was positive.

Breck was suddenly aware that Jane was eyeing him curiously.

"Your thoughts are miles and miles away," she accused.

"I was thinking about you—and things," he told her soberly.

"You mean—"

"The breaks were all against us—that night in Calico. Ramon Matute could have told us a lot—given us a lead." Breck started the gray down the trail. "Ramon was killed by somebody who was afraid we'd learn too much from him."

"It's mysterious, where Mr. Stamper has gone —without telling anybody," mused the girl. Her tone was thoughtful. "You know, Breck, I can't forget that strange look he gave me when I asked him why he called his ranch the Horseshoe. It was on the tip of my tongue to ask him if he had ever heard of the Lost Horseshoe Mine."

"It might explain his interest in Mexican Wells," pondered Breck. "There's something in that country he wants—and wants badly."

"A lost gold mine, for instance," Jane conjectured.

"A lost gold mine," agreed Breck. "It's possible, Jane." He looked at her, wondered at her oddly tense expression.

"Is there really such a gold mine?" she queried abruptly. "Is there really such a thing as the

Horseshoe Lode? Have you *ever* heard of it, Breck? I've been wondering—"

"I got a yarn about it from old Jim Hawker," he admitted. "Sort of legend, Jim says. He doesn't take much stock in it."

"What's the story?" demanded Jane impatiently. "What does Jim say?"

"Oh, the usual old-time yarn about a prospector found dying of thirst in the desert—has his pack loaded with rich gold nuggets . . . claims he's made the biggest gold strike in history . . . dies before he can tell anything more, or where his mine is located."

"How does the Horseshoe come into the story?" Jane wanted to know. "Why is it called the Horseshoe Lode?"

"That's the queer part of the yarn," Breck went on. "There was a crude map in his pocket, showing what appeared to be the mouth of a canyon. Jim said he saw the map years ago when he happened to be in Stovepipe Wells. An old desert rat was carrying it around in his pocket and trying to get him a grubstake. Jim said the mouth of this canyon was shaped like a horseshoe."

"It sounds quite possible," Jane declared. "And Jim did see this map." Excitement flushed her cheeks. "Breck! I've an idea that Val Stamper has that old map!"

"I'm beginning to think he has something that's got him crazy," agreed Breck.

"Don't you see?" she cried. "Val Stamper has possession of that prospector's map and in some way has managed to read its secret—"

"Which explains why he wants Mexican Wells and the Cactus Hills range," Breck broke in. "Somewhere in those hills is a canyon with an entrance shaped like a horseshoe—only old Val hasn't been able to locate the canyon—"

"It's the only answer," Jane persisted. "I'll tell you why I think so, Breck." Her low voice faltered. "That scrap of paper I showed you—from my father's diary . . . Doesn't it mean anything to you?"

"Your friend, Dr. Wingate, got it from a prospector, who found it in a shack in the Funeral Mountains," Breck said slowly.

"It was dated at Mexican Wells," the girl pointed out, "and there is a reference to the Lost Horseshoe Lode—to the Painted Canyon." Jane's voice broke. "It—it's the last word we—we've had of him—and it proves that he actually was at Mexican Wells and planned to explore the Painted Canyon."

"How did that piece of paper ever find its way back to Death Valley—to the Funeral Mountains?" puzzled Breck.

"Some person must have found his diary and carried it away, some prospector who thought it would be valuable," Jane guessed. Her voice was unsteady.

Breck read what was in her mind. The picture of her father—dead, or dying, in that savage, inhospitable desert, perhaps slain by those who also sought to solve the secret of the lost lode.

"The scrap of diary mentions a companion—a man named Pete," he reminded. "It is possible that Pete escaped, and took your father's diary with him, planning to return some day and have another try for the lost mine."

"I think that is what happened," Jane agreed quietly. "Pete went back to his shack in the Funeral Mountains and hid the diary under the floor boards—"

"You're getting the picture." Breck nodded. "I can see them—your father—this Pete—"

"Something happened to Pete," pursued the girl. "He died or something . . . at least he never returned to his shack . . . and the rats chewed up the diary—and one day another prospector was at the shack and found this torn page,"—she touched her breast—"and he kept it, because being a prospector those few words would rouse his interest—"

"You're doing splendidly," encouraged Breck. "The picture grows—"

"—and then Dr. Wingate found this prospector dying—bitten by a rattlesnake—and because Dr. Wingate was kind to him and tried to help him, this prospector gave him the piece of diary to show his gratitude and because he thought it might lead Dr. Wingate to the lost Horseshoe Lode."

"The picture is almost complete," muttered Breck. "Does it grow, still more, Jane—"

Her face was pale. "I'm afraid," she said faintly. "I'm afraid to go any further, Breck. I begin to see a face—"

"Val Stamper's face?" Breck's tone was bleak. "You see Val Stamper's face—"

Jane nodded miserably. "Why did those men try to drive me from Mexican Wells?" she asked in a low voice, "why did they try to murder me—in the Painted Canyon?"

"Somebody didn't want you there," Breck said grimly.

"Val Stamper didn't want me there," she declared. "You say he's wanted to possess Mexican Wells—the Cactus Hills—for years. He murdered my father—to keep him away from the lost mine he has been searching for himself.

"It is all too dreadful!" cried the girl. "This lost mine has driven Val Stamper mad, and when he learned that I was at Mexican Wells, he suspected my purpose—tried to have me and Aunt Sally killed."

"It's a terrible accusation," muttered Breck. "We mustn't let our imaginations run away with us, Jane."

"I asked him point blank what it was he wanted at Mexican Wells," reminded the girl.

"He refused to tell me—offered me five thousand dollars to go away and never come back."

"There may be others who are looking for the lost mine," argued Breck.

"The man who tried to frighten me from Mexican Wells rode horses that carried his brand," Jane again reminded. "Val Stamper did not deny they were his horses. He could only say that he had no knowledge of the matter. I believed him at first—but now I am sure he is responsible for all these dreadful things—even for your father's murder."

"I wish I knew." Breck's tone was brittle.

"You have been away for seven years," Jane pointed out. "Your father may have learned things about the Horseshoe Lode. If it is true that Val Stamper killed my father—he would keep on killing—as a madman would keep on killing."

"We'll both be crazy, if we think about it any more today," Breck said harshly. "Put the thing out of your mind, Jane. You've drawn the picture —as far as Val Stamper. Let it rest there until we can be sure of the finish." He gestured. "Look!"

The desert reached before them, serene and lovely, flushed with the changing lights and shadows of eventide. They reined their horses.

"It's beautiful," whispered the girl. "The savagery, the harshness, is gone. The desert at sunset! I love it, Breck!"

A lone horseman swung into view from behind

a saffron-tinted dune. Breck reached for his binoculars and studied the rider intently.

"Bowie Smith," he announced. "Jim said Bowie was coming to the ranch tonight for a talk." He lowered the glasses. "Wonder why Bill and Ned Gorman aren't with him. Jim said they'd be along with Bowie."

"Perhaps they live too far apart to be riding the same trail to the Circle B," suggested the girl.

"That's the point," Breck answered. "Bowie Smith's Lazy S takes in most of the South Fork of the Calico. He's a close neighbor to their G Bar G outfit. Looks like Bill and Ned are not coming to the talk-fest, or they'd be trailing along with Bowie.

"It's Bowie, all right. I know that slash bay he rides—" Breck broke off with a startled exclamation, and Jane too, saw the twin puffs of smoke curl from a mesquite bush, saw the approaching rider collapse from his saddle. Faintly the gunshots touched their shocked ears.

"They've shot him!" gasped the girl. "Somebody's shot him—" She stared at Breck with dilated eyes.

He was hurriedly jerking rifle from saddle-boot.

"Jane—make dust back to the ranch . . . tell Jim to come on the jump with the boys—" He sent the gray into a dead run down the long slope.

Jane hesitated, reluctant to ride back to the ranch and leave him to face the unknown assassins alone. She heard a shout from the rimrock above and turned startled eyes. Johnny Wing and Dusty Rodes were coming at reckless speed down the precipitous descent.

The astonished girl pulled the brown mare off the trail and let them go by. Gravel from flying hoofs showered her. It was not hard for Jane to guess why the two cowboys were so opportunely at hand. Old Jim Hawker was not taking chances. He feared another tragedy—such as had over-taken his old boss.

She hesitated no longer, sent the brown mare racing down the slope.

The big gray horse far in the lead, slid to a snorting halt alongside the limp form sprawled in the lengthening shade of a greasewood. Breck flung himself from the saddle and stooped over the bearded ranchman's inert body. A brief look told him that the Lazy S man was still breathing. In the distance beyond he could hear the quick beat of hoofs as the killers fled into the sunset. Two riders, he judged by the sound.

Bowie Smith opened his eyes. It was plain to Breck that his moments to live were brief. He pillowed the dying man's head in his arms.

"They—they got me—Breck . . . like they got yore dad—" The bearded lips moved in an effort to speak.

"Who did it, Bowie?"

"You'd be—surprised, Breck—"

Life was ebbing fast from Bowie Smith. He desperately wanted to tell Breck something—something of vast importance. His breath came in painful gasps, blew flecks of blood on his tawny-gray beard.

". . . found out today . . . yore dad . . . it—it was—was—"

The Lazy S man sighed deeply, relaxed in the young cattleman's arms.

Breck turned a bleak face to Johnny Wing and Dusty Rodes as they tumbled from their saddles.

"Who done it, boss?" Johnny's voice crackled. "Doggone!" he added bitterly. "Bowie Smith . . . it's good ol' Bowie they done killed—"

The two cowboys exchanged dismayed looks.

"Did he talk, boss, before he cashed in? Did Bowie get a look at them coyotes?"

"He was trying to tell me, Johnny—"

Breck gently lowered Bowie Smith's stiffening form to the earth and got to his feet.

"He was killed because he'd found out who murdered my father—"

Breck's voice was unsteady, and he went slowly toward the white-faced girl scrambling from her saddle.

Chapter Ten

The Gormans

Jane watched with fascinated eyes from a shadowed corner of the ranch office. She was reminded of a painting she had seen somewhere, men's faces, vaguely showing through the swirling smoke of a council fire, hard, grim faces, like the faces of these men grouped around Breck Allen.

He sat in the creaky swivel chair, his profile etched in stern, harsh lines against the dim light of the kerosene lamp on the desk at his back.

Old Jim Hawker was there, his chair tilted against the wall, and side by side near the door, Johnny Wing and Dusty Rodes, sitting on their heels, their cigarettes making twin ruby eyes in the semi-darkness. Two others sat loosely on a wooden bench against the wall opposite Breck. Bill Gorman and his brother Ned, the owners of the G Bar G. There was a dejected sag to the shoulders of these two former members of the Circle B outfit.

"We figgered Bowie would wait for us," Bill, the elder of the brothers, repeated for the third time. "We stopped in at the Lazy S like we promised—found Bowie had started out for yore place—"

"Who told yuh Bowie was headed this way?" Jim Hawker's voice was gruff. The dead cattleman was an old friend.

"Why, there weren't nobody home, Jim," broke in Ned Gorman. "You know how Bowie lived by his lonesome."

The Circle B foreman nodded. It was true that Bowie Smith lived alone. He was a bachelor—did his own cooking.

"Where was his boys?" he wanted to know. "Pete and Denny—"

"I reckon Pete an' Denny was down at Bowie's Cat Canyon camp," explained Bill Gorman. "Bowie told us he figgered to throw that bunch of three-year-olds in with yore trail herd."

"That's right," confirmed his brother. "He'd some twenty head of three-year-olds, Bowie told us he aimed to ship before they was rustled off of him. Reckon Pete an' Denny was combin' 'em out of the brakes."

Jim Hawker nodded again. "I told Bowie he could throw 'em in with our herd," he admitted. "He planned to short-cut through Cat Canyon and meet us this side of Shoshone Pass."

Breck spoke thoughtfully. "It's strange Bowie didn't wait for you boys. He'd arranged for you to meet him at his place."

"Shore too bad he didn't wait," muttered Ned Gorman. A match flared in his fingers. His face was haggard under the brief flicker of light.

Jane's eyes pitied him. The poor fellow was feeling dreadfully, and his brother. They were visibly shaken by the tragedy. Jane was sorry for them. The Gorman brothers were nice men— former Circle B hands, Breck had told her. His father had set them up in the cattle business, supplied them with the beginnings of their herd. With the rest of the decent cattlemen, the brothers had suffered severely at the hands of the rustlers. She continued to study them from her darkened corner. They were not a type attractive to her, despite Breck's assertion of their trustworthiness. There was something definitely hard about their faces, and the elder brother, Bill, had a curious way of staring at the toes of his boots when talking.

"What do you aim to do 'bout this killin', Breck?" Another match flared in Ned Gorman's fingers. The G Bar G man was having trouble keeping his cigarette alight. Matches littered the floor at his feet. It was plain to the others that panic gripped the younger Gorman. "We got to do somethin'—quick," he said hoarsely. "No tellin' who's next on the list! Might be me—or Bill—or yoreself, Breck—"

"No sense for yuh to get stampeded," muttered his brother. He stared down at his boots. "Ned's right, at that, Breck. We got to act quick— and I reckon it's up to you to sort of take charge of things." He looked briefly at the young Circle

B owner's stern, inscrutable face. "Any idee who done the killin'? You was up on the slope—and saw the shootin'."

"We saw the shooting, Bill—" Breck shook his head. "The killers got away from there fast."

"Didn't yuh see them makin' their getaway?" persisted Bill Gorman. "Didn't yuh find no tracks, nor nothin'—back in the mesquite where they was hid?"

"How did you know the killers were hiding in the mesquite, Bill?"

The G Bar G man shrugged his dusty shoulders. "They'd be hidin' some place near the trail," he said sourly. "Wish I'd been along with yuh to look for their tracks."

"They were too smart to leave their cards behind them." Breck fingered two empty rifle shells in his pocket. They were .44's. The bullet that had snuffed the life from old Breck Allen had been a .44. "They got away from there fast, Bill," he repeated. "Didn't even get a look at their horses."

Johnny Wing and Dusty Rodes exchanged looks. They both knew of the two empty rifle shells in Breck's pocket. Johnny had found them in the mesquite where the murderers had lain in wait for Bowie Smith.

"We saw the shootin' from the rimrock, Bill," Johnny said. "It's like the boss tells yuh. Them sneakin' coyotes lost themselves awful quick in the chaparral."

Bill Gorman shook his head. "Purty slick *hombres*—not to leave no tracks—no clue—"

"Cold-blooded murder," croaked Jim Hawker. "Somebody knew Bowie was headed this way and lay for him."

"Was he dead when yuh got to him, Breck?" The elder Gorman darted another brief glance at the Circle B owner. "Mebbe Bowie was able to talk some—before he—he—"

"I told you all I know about the killing, Bill." Breck's tone was curt. "What do you boys plan to do? Bunk down here for the night? You're welcome—"

Johnny and Dusty stared at him, their poker faces impassive. Jane sensed they were mystified by something Breck had said—or failed to say.

"Well—" Bill Gorman's eyes questioned his brother. "What yuh say, Ned? Don't yuh figger we should get word to Pete and Denny?"

"Bowie can't ship them steers now he's dead," muttered the younger G Bar G man. "Seems like we should let Pete and Denny know—"

"The sheriff should know, too," Bill reminded the others.

"I've sent word to Clem," Breck told him. "He'll be out by dawn—if not sooner."

"No good for us to hang around," Bill Gorman decided. "We didn't see the shootin' and can't be any help to the sheriff." He rose from the bench. "Well—let's fork our broncs, Ned. It's up to us to let Pete and Denny know about poor Bowie."

"I can send one of the boys over to Cat Canyon," Breck suggested. "Maybe you and Ned would like to stay over for the inquest. Clem will bring the coroner with him."

"Reckon not, Breck." The G Bar G man turned to the door. "Nothin' we can do. Might as well mosey along back. We can help Pete and Denny 'tend to things at the Lazy S." He eyed round at Breck. "Let us know when yuh got some plan figgered out. Ned and me shore want to throw in with yuh on this deal. Won't be no peace for us till we get these rustlers on the run."

Jim Hawker followed the Gormans outside. "You boys have come a long way," he reminded. "Why don't yuh throw yore saddles on a couple fresh broncs? Plenty in the corral. You can pick up yore broncs next time yuh come round—"

Bill Gorman thanked him, but said he reckoned their horses were good for the ride home. Their boots crunched across the yard to the hitch-rail under a cottonwood.

Johnny Wing's eyes signaled the dark-faced Dusty Rodes. They stood up, eyes mutely questioning their boss.

"What's on your mind, Johnny?" There was a curious note in Breck's voice.

"Was sort of wonderin', boss—" Johnny hesitated, threw Jane an embarrassed grin. "Well, you wasn't sayin' much to Bill and Ned—"

"Not much to say, Johnny."

Johnny moved reluctantly toward the door. Jane read dissatisfaction, some bewilderment in his honest blue eyes. He stepped into the starlit night. Dusty followed him.

The Gorman brothers were riding toward the high swing gate beyond the horse corral. Johnny Wing's gaze followed them thoughtfully.

"What's on yore mind, cowboy?" queried Dusty. "You've got that funny look yuh wear when yuh're tryin' to think."

Johnny moved on across the yard.

"What's the idee?" grumbled his dark-faced companion. "Bunk house don't lay over there."

"Just a notion I got," Johnny said briefly. "I crave to study hoofprints. I'm awful cur'ous about hoofprints, Dusty. I'm makin' a close study about hoofprints. Mebbe I'll write me a book about 'em."

"Me, too," muttered Dusty Rodes. "I can think as quick as you can, feller."

"You an' me is like Breck—when it comes to quick thinkin'," Johnny said grimly.

"Bill an' Ned were awful broke up about Bowie Smith," observed Dusty. "Ned's hands were shaking so bad he couldn't light his cigarette. Acted like he was scared plumb to death."

"Breck kept quiet about them two rifle cartridges we found under that mesquite," Johnny murmured. "Did yuh notice, Dusty, how the boss let Bill an' Ned do all the talkin'?"

"Bill seemed awful anxious to know about tracks," Dusty said softly. "Why didn't the boss tell him about them tracks we found, feller? Why didn't Breck tell Bill that one of the broncs was wearin' a broke shoe on the off hind foot?"

Johnny halted and eyed his companion. "You take a page from Breck's book, feller," he said meaningly. "You an' me has notions, but we're goin' to be awful close-mouthed about 'em— like the boss—"

Jim Hawker's tall form loomed out of the darkness.

"Where you boys headed?" he wanted to know. "You'd better get some sleep, Dusty, while Johnny keeps watch at the house. It's turn an' turn about for yuh." The old foreman's voice was worried. "I'm depending on yuh to look out for Breck. You ain't lettin' him—nor the gal—out of yore sight—"

"You bet, Jim," chorused the cowboys earnestly. "Don't worry about us. We're on the job," Johnny added.

Hawker continued on his way back to the ranch office. Johnny's glance followed the tall, stooped form.

"Jim's awful jumpy," he told his companion.

"He's got it figgered Breck's due for the next bullet."

"Too dark to see hoof-marks," Dusty grumbled as they paused at the long hitch-rack under the cottonwood tree. "It's a job for daylight."

Reluctantly they postponed the study of hoof-prints and followed Jim Hawker back to the ranch office.

The lamp winked out and Breck and Jane emerged from the door. There was a puzzled look in the face the girl lifted to her tall companion.

"Breck, I'm like Johnny—wondering, too—"

He smiled down at her, shrugged his shoulders.

"You didn't tell those men all we know," she persisted. "Why didn't you, Breck? Don't you trust the Gormans?"

Breck stared frowningly at the approaching forms of Jim Hawker and the two cowboys.

"I'm not entirely satisfied with their story," he finally admitted. "Don't ask me why, Jane." He fingered the two empty .44 cartridges in his pocket.

"I'm frightened," murmured the girl. "The Gorman men are old Circle B riders. You told me you trusted them."

"I'm beginning to wonder," he muttered unhappily. "Give me time, Jane. There's a mystery here—and right now I don't see the answer."

Chapter Eleven

Aunt Sally Interrupts

The bawling of the trail herd awoke Jane. She threw back the covers and sat up. The dawn showed pale through the wide-open windows. Jim Hawker was getting an early start for the drive.

Jane reached for her slippers and padded into the bathroom. A quick, cold splash might repair the ravages of a restless night. She had slept badly, harassed by dreams, the bearded face of the slain Lazy S rancher, the naked, vulturine head of Val Stamper poking over her bedside and demanding that she tell him what it was she hoped to find in the Painted Canyon. She had tried to scream and suddenly the leering face was a hideous buzzard, perched on her chest and beating her with sable wings and picking at her eyes. Shrill cries answered her screams and Breck miraculously appeared, six-guns spurting flame. Jane had awakened then, but the shrill yells still sounded in her ears, the yipping of cowboys pushing the great herd from the corrals.

The shock of the cold water cooled and refreshed her. She rubbed herself dry and hurriedly dressed. Breck had said something about going with the trail herd in Jim Hawker's place. She wanted to have a talk with Breck.

She pulled on her white Stetson, and after a moment's thought buckled on her gun-holster. There was something reassuring in the light press of that .32 against her hip.

He aunt's door opened as she went quietly down the hall. The old lady peered at her suspiciously.

"You needn't be afraid of wakening me," she assured the girl. "As if anybody could sleep with all that bellowing and yelling; and where do you think you are going, young woman? Seems to me there's always trouble when you go round wearing those cowboy clothes—and that horrid gun—"

"I want to see them start the cattle on the drive," Jane explained. "I may ride as far as Deer Creek with them—if Breck goes."

"He's having his breakfast now," Aunt Sally informed her. "I'll be down myself in a few minutes for a cup of coffee. I might as well be enjoying a sunrise as pretending to be asleep."

"Yes, dear auntie," smiled the girl. "You'll have to hurry if you plan to breakfast with Breck and me." She hurried down the stairs and out to the patio where she knew Benito would be serving Breck his bacon and eggs and coffee.

Surprise was in the look he gave her as he rose from his chair.

"*Buenas dias, Señor,*" she greeted. "Is it not kind of me to brighten your sunrise breakfast table with my presence?" She sank into the chair opposite him and gestured gaily at the rose-flushed horizon. "The divine hour of all the hours," she declared. "It is too stupid to stay in bed—miss the splendor of the dawn."

His frowning gaze was taking in her garb and it was apparent that her enthusiasm over the sunrise was in no way making him subjective to her will.

"Just where do you think you are going?" he wanted to know in a chilly tone.

"You're nothing but an old echo," complained Jane. "Aunt Sally asked the same question in almost the same words. You might at least be original and ask 'where in blazes are yuh headed for, mister?'"

Breck grinned. "You'd better get outside of your breakfast in a hurry—if you're riding along with us," he surrendered.

"Let 'er buck, mister," laughed the girl. "I'm right with yuh!"

Benito bore down on them with bacon and eggs and a pot of coffee.

"Are you going all the way?" queried Jane.

He shook his head. "Only as far as Deer Creek. I'll have to be here when Clem Sorrel and the coroner come."

Jane was frankly relieved by the news. "I was

hoping you wouldn't go with the trail herd," she confessed. "It's not safe for you—*any-where*—except here at the house—until the mystery of these murderous attacks are solved."

"You can't expect me to hide like a frightened rabbit in its hole," Breck pointed out dryly. "After all, I'm supposed to be running the affairs of this ranch."

"It's silly of me," Jane murmured. She toyed nervously with her coffee spoon. "I've had the horrid thought that it was *you* those men planned to shoot—and not Bowie Smith—"

"No," Breck said. "It was Bowie they wanted this time."

"But they won't stop until they get you," worried the girl. "Jim Hawker is all jumpy about you—or he wouldn't have Johnny and Dusty always dogging your heels."

"You're letting it get you," grumbled Breck. "Forget it . . . eat your breakfast—if you want to ride with us to Deer Creek."

"Well, at least you're not going through Shoshone Pass with the cattle," Jane said with a little sigh.

"Not so fast," chuckled Breck. "As soon as Clem Sorrel and the coroner finish with this business I'm riding after the herd. I'll overtake the outfit this side of Shoshone Pass. Not fair to leave it to old Jim. It's all up with the Circle B Ranch if those cattle don't get to market."

Jane gave him a dismayed look, saw that further protests would only annoy him.

"When will you be back?" she inquired in a low voice.

"Inside of a week."

"I may not be here," Jane mused.

His eyes widened at her.

"Aunt Sally and I must either return to Mexican Wells—or I must give up my plans entirely," she explained. "You have trouble enough—without me to worry about."

"You will stay here at the ranch until I get back!" Breck glowered at her. "You'll keep away from Mexican Wells." His face softened. "I won't stand for nesters on Circle B range," he added with a placating smile.

Jane's mutinous mouth relaxed to its customary lovely curves.

"It's only that I don't want to be one more burden for you to shoulder," she said. "If I could do something to help, I'd feel better." She gestured impatiently. "I wish I were a man—"

"I'm glad you are just *Jane,*" he interrupted in a low voice. There was a wistfulness, a longing in his gray eyes that startled her, held her breathless. "I'm glad you are not a man, Jane!"

She colored, met his look squarely. "Are you, Breck?"

"More than you know!" Breck's voice was

unsteady. "There have been compensations for me out of all this trouble."

"Compensations, Breck?" She smiled demurely, lowered long dark lashes.

"You—your friendship," he said a bit doggedly, "knowing you, Jane—and—"

"You look very serious, you two young people," broke in the vivacious voice of Aunt Sally. "Don't tell me if it's more bad news about somebody else being murdered. I must have my coffee first."

"No, Auntie, it's not bad news—" There was an odd, singing note in the girl's low voice and she flashed a quick bright smile at the young man opposite her. "Breck is feeling very hopeful about things this morning and sees a rainbow in the clouds."

"Well,"—Aunt Sally settled her plump person into a chair—"I'd like to see a rainbow in this desert country. I'm beginning to wonder if a drop of rain ever falls on the Circle B range."

"You'll see plenty in a month or two," Breck assured her. "Comes in cloudbursts. First thing you know that desert"—he waved a hand—"will be all the colors of a rainbow. You be patient and you'll see more wild flowers than you ever dreamed of."

"I don't care for fairy tales before I have my coffee," complained the old lady.

The soft-footed Benito glided into the patio

with his tray. Aunt Sally beamed. "Here comes *my* rainbow," she chuckled.

They left her contentedly at her breakfast and went into the yard. Beyond the corrals lifted the dust banner of the trail herd, moving slowly across the brown slopes. Johnny Wing and Dusty Rodes were intently scrutinizing the trampled earth by the hitch-rail under the cottonwood tree.

"What in the world are those boys looking for," wondered Jane. "They must have lost something—"

"Studying hoof-marks," Breck told her grimly.

"Hoof-marks!" Jane wrinkled her brows. "Why, Breck?"

"One of the horses ridden by those killers wore a broken shoe. Johnny and Dusty are curious about that horse—"

"Oh!" Jane gave him a worried look. "You *do* suspect the Gorman brothers, then—"

"I hope I'm wrong." Breck's eyes were bleak.

"I'm sure you are wrong," averred Jane. "Those men wouldn't do such a dreadful thing. Why, they used to work for the Circle B. You've known them for years."

The two cowboys approached with the short, stiff-legged gait of their kind. Johnny shook his head at the question in Breck's eyes.

"No pay-dirt there," he announced briefly, with an admiring smile for the girl. "Ridin' with us, ma'am?"

"As far as Deer Creek, Johnny."

"*Muy bueno*," grinned the cowboy. "Dusty, you mind yore language now a lady's along with us."

The taciturn Dusty gave his loquacious fellow-rider a dark look. There was something formidable about the swarthy little man. Jane found it hard to really like him as she did the irrepressible Johnny. His expression was changeless, always bleak, and he had a way of looking at her with unwinking, narrowed eyes. Breck assured her that it was Dusty's habitual poker face. Dusty was never known to get excited. He was all ice and his hands could reach for those low-slung guns with the speed of forked lightning. Old Jim Hawker had chosen Breck's bodyguard with canny wisdom, the girl gratefully reflected.

The plan to accompany the trail herd to Deer Creek was disrupted by the arrival of Sheriff Sorrel and the coroner.

"Come as quick as I heard the news, Breck," said the old law-officer. He climbed stiffly from the buckboard. "Fetched Doc Stevens along."

He indicated the stout man dozing in the seat. "Doc's been up three nights' runnin' . . . two babies in Spanish Town—and a shootin' scrape in Bart Cordy's joint." He shook the coroner's dusty, alpaca shoulder. "Wake up, Doc!"

The stout coroner blinked drowsy eyes at the faces looking at him.

"What a life," he grumbled. "You've no mercy

on a sawbones, Clem. No sense dragging me out here to look at a dead man. I'll be dead myself if I don't get some sleep."

"You and Clem better have breakfast, first," suggested Breck as the doctor extricated his bulk from the dusty buckboard.

Doc Stevens brightened visibly. Breakfast, and strong black coffee would make a new man of him, he declared. His genial smile went to the girl by Breck's side.

"Well, well!" he ejaculated. "I didn't know you'd taken a wife, Breck!"

The young Circle B man reddened, and there was a chuckle from Johnny Wing.

"You mustn't jump to conclusions, Doc," grinned Sheriff Sorrel. "Give the boy a chance. He ain't knowed Miss Tallant more'n a week or two."

Breck glared at him, conscious of Jane's amused smile.

"Tallant!" Doc Stevens eyed the girl with evident interest. "I've heard that name—"

"My father was Professor Tallant," Jane told him.

The doctor nodded. "Ah—I remember. He was lost somewhere in Death Valley, the papers said. So you are his daughter. Well, well! A very mysterious business, your father's disappearance, Miss Tallant—"

Breck saw the girl's eyes darken with excitement —a sudden hope.

"Why don't you take Doc to the patio and see

about his breakfast?" he suggested. "The ride to Deer Creek is off. Too late by the time we're finished with the inquest."

Jane went off with the doctor readily enough, buoyed by the hope she might glean some news from him.

"Tell Benito to fix up some ham and eggs for Clem, too," Breck called after her.

The lanky sheriff's face was grave as he looked at the young cattleman.

"Val Stamper's still missing," he said. "Kirk Bannion's getting worried, and Della—she's throwing fits about it."

"Queer business," admitted Breck. "Have they tried Las Vegas? Val Stamper does a lot of banking there—"

"He ain't been there, 'cordin' to what Kirk says," answered the sheriff. "Well, tell me 'bout this killin'. Any notion who done poor Bowie Smith in?"

Breck related all the facts that he knew about the murder.

"Bowie tried to tell me something important he'd found out—something about the shooting of my father—"

Clem Sorrel listened attentively.

"Looks like he was killed to stop him from talkin'," he agreed.

"Bowie was killed by the men who murdered dad," declared Breck.

He showed the sheriff the two empty .44 cartridges found by Johnny Wing at the scene of the ambush.

"It was a .44 that killed dad," he reminded.

"It kind of proves Val Stamper had no hand in yore dad's murder," mused the old law-officer. "Val's been missing a week, now. It's this rustler gang, Breck. Yore dad was shot because he'd learned who the boss rustler was, and Bowie Smith was ambushed for the same reason."

"Bowie said I would be surprised," recalled Breck. "The man back of this rustler gang must be somebody we all know—and trust." He smiled thinly. "Bowie saying that has got me suspecting everybody—even the Gorman brothers—"

The sheriff gave him an astonished look. "Hell, no!" he protested. "Bill an' Ned Gorman ain't the kind to run with rustlers and killers, Breck. You're loco if yuh think that of 'em. I've knowed those boys all their lives. They worked for yore dad—" His gaze went to the patio gate. "You said something about breakfast—an' coffee," he grinned.

They moved toward the gate, and Breck said thoughtfully, "You claim that because Val Stamper was already missing when Bowie Smith was shot, proves he had no hand in the killing—and the other killings."

"That's the way I figger it," admitted the sheriff.

"I figure it different," Breck said grimly. "How

do we know that Val Stamper isn't with the rustler gang at this moment—at their secret hideout."

The suggestion visibly startled Sheriff Sorrel.

"Why, Breck . . . mebbe we *don't* know," he worried. "It's an awful mess—"

"If we could get hold of the right string, we'd soon untangle the mystery," mused Breck. "I've a hunch there's a link that ties up this rustling with Val Stamper's obsession to own the Cactus Hills range."

The veteran law-officer nodded. "Bowie Smith said you'd be some surprised—when you got hold of that tangled string," he muttered. "Well, there's the doc—ready for the inquest—"

Doc Stevens made brief work of the inquest and midmorning saw Bowie Smith laid to rest in a grave not far from that of Breck's slain father.

"Bowie had no kin that I ever heard of," Sheriff Sorrel pointed out. "I'm thinkin' your dad would like to have him lay there. Bowie was an old friend." He climbed into the buckboard. "Get in," he said to Doc Stevens. "I'll give you a lift back to town."

The buckboard rattled away in a cloud of dust. Breck saddled his horse, then went to find Jane. He was wondering what she had learned from Doc Stevens.

"Not a thing—that helps," the girl told him. Her tone was despondent. The brief funeral service had left her in low spirits. Death seemed to lurk behind every bush. The sight of those several newly-made graves was profoundly disturbing.

She shook her head. "The doctor thinks it's hopeless . . . keeping up the search for Dad. He says that Dad undoubtedly met his end in Death Valley and that after all these years I cannot hope to learn what happened. Of course, I didn't tell him about the diary."

"Don't mention it to anybody," counseled Breck. "It's our secret—for the present."

Jane looked longingly at the tall gray horse.

"I'd like to be going with you," she said.

"Not this trip." He eyed her sternly. "You stick close to the house . . . no riding off alone," he warned.

She promised. Breck stepped up to his saddle, smiled down at her.

"*Adios, Señorita—*"

"*Adios, Señor—*" Her voice was low, a bit unsteady. "Don't be gone too long, Breck."

"*Hasta la vista,* Jane—"

His hand lifted in a parting gesture, and suddenly Jane was alone under the trees, watching the man she loved ride away. She knew now that she loved Breck . . . knew that he loved her. She stood, watching, until horse and rider dropped from view down the canyon trail.

Chapter Twelve

Sunset Shadows

Evening shadows were drawing up the canyon slopes when Breck reached the Lazy S, in the south fork of the Calico. He had promised Clem Sorrel he would see Pete and Denny and tell them the result of the inquest. They were first-rate men and he wanted them on the Circle B payroll as soon as Bowie Smith's affairs were settled. The winding up of the slain rancher's estate would be simple, according to the sheriff. The few remaining cattle would go to Val Stamper's bank, together with all that went with the Lazy S ranch.

There was no sign of Pete and Denny. Corrals and barns were empty. There was a forlornness about the place that depressed Breck.

He took a look inside the log cabin Bowie Smith had reared on the banks of the Little Calico. Dust-drift from an open window lay on the floor, unmarked by boot-prints. No man had entered since the rancher's departure twenty-four hours earlier.

Breck went back to his horse. There was something wrong. Pete and Denny should have been around. Bill Gorman had said he would tell them of Bowie Smith's murder. It was possible the Lazy S men had fled, fearing a similar fate.

Breck discarded the explanation. Pete and Denny were not quitters. Something had happened to them.

He swung into the trail that followed the twisting course of the Little Calico. He would have a look at the Lazy S round-up camp. It was possible the Gormans had failed to notify the boys of Bowie Smith's death. He could push on through the Cat Canyon short-cut and overtake the trail herd at Indian Flats. He knew Jim Hawker would bed the herd for the night at the flats. The feed was good, with plenty of water in Shoshone Creek. He could easily make Indian Flats by midnight.

Sunset lay yellow on the mesa above the creek.

Breck reined the gray horse, conscious of a cold prickle of dismay. The camp was deserted— no living creature visible, save a buzzard that winged reluctantly away from the corral fence. He knew that death had again struck at the Lazy S.

He rode on past the pole corral, eyes alert for what he sought.

Pete Ogram lay face down in the chaparral, a gun clutched in stiffened fingers. A hundred yards along the trail was the lifeless body of Denny Murphy.

They had died with their guns smoking in a

valiant attempt to save Bowie Smith's little herd from the rustlers.

There was nothing Breck could do save carry the slain Lazy S men into the camp cabin, out of reach of coyotes and buzzards.

The sunlight was fading when finally he rode on his way to the Gormans' G Bar G, five miles up the creek. The detour to the Gormans would delay him more than two hours, but the brothers were nearest neighbors to the Lazy S. Bill and Ned must be told of these latest killings. They could care for the dead men and notify the sheriff.

New fears troubled Breck as he rode through the fast-growing darkness. The rustlers were obviously well informed—were aware of Bowie Smith's plan to throw in his little herd with the Circle B drive. In which case the Circle B trail herd was also likely marked for a raid. Spies were busy in the Calico country.

He pushed the gray horse along as fast as the rough trail permitted. It had been years since he had last ridden so far up the Little Calico. It was a wild and remote district, with the notorious Pot Holes lying to the south. Honest men avoided the Pot Holes. The tortuous maze of canyons afforded ideal hideouts for rustlers and desperadoes. Breck guessed that it was in some hidden valley in the Pot Holes that the rustlers kept the stolen cattle until they could be moved with safety to some distant market.

Breck's thoughts went to Val Stamper. The banker's strange disappearance added to the baffling mystery. He disliked Della's father for a greedy, unscrupulous man, but he was finding it hard to believe that Val Stamper was the instigator of this wholesale cow-stealing—the killings. The old buzzard-faced owner of the Horseshoe was without mercy in his financial dealings—but he would not stoop to murder. There was no ques-tion of his curious interest in Mexican Wells. There was something in the Cactus Hills the man wanted—an obsession of years standing. Breck was convinced now that Val Stamper's dominating desire was to find the lost Horseshoe Lode. He was also convinced that another shared the same desire—that it was this mysterious unknown who had sent his men to murder Jane Tallant. The three men he had battled that afternoon rode horses wearing the Horseshoe brand. The Horse-shoe foreman had admitted that Ramon Matute was on the Horseshoe pay-roll, and Kirk Bannion had appeared at the jail declaring Val Stamper wanted the man bailed out.

Breck recalled the scene on the porch of Mat Haley's hotel. Al Roan and the lawyer had heard Breck announce his determination to force a confession from the Mexican. Within the hour Ramon Matute was dead, a knife in his throat. It was those several incidents of Ramon's capture in the street, his murder in the jail, that had first fastened Breck's attention on Kirk Bannion and the Horseshoe foreman. He doubted the lawyer's story of Val Stamper's wish to have the Mexican freed on bail.

The lawyer was obviously high in the banker's favor—had his confidence. It was possible the old man had in some way accidentally betrayed his long-cherished secret of the lost gold mine. Kirk Bannion was shrewd, as cunning as any fox. He possessed the sort of brains that could organize a gang of desperadoes and successfully direct their lawless operations.

Breck had learned a few things about the man from Tonio, the Shoshone half-breed who had wed one of Jose Moraga's numerous daughters. Bannion was often at Jose Moraga's cantina, as was Al Roan. Under the circumstances Breck was suspicious of the friendly relations between the lawyer and the Horseshoe foreman. He believed that old Val Stamper would have been astonished had he known of these secret meetings in Moraga's *cantina*.

There had been little else Tonio could tell Breck about Kirk Bannion. Nor did the Shoshone half-breed agree that the man was a Mexican. A *Californio*, perhaps, was Tonio's assertion, probably from Los Angeles.

The Shoshone half-breed was probably right, Breck reflected. Kirk Bannion was either a high-caste Mexican, or a descendant of one of the old

Spanish-Californian families. Whatever he was, or wherever he was from, the man was on his black list of suspects.

Breck thought with misgivings of his talk with Bannion. He should not have shown his hand—put the man on his guard, especially at this time when he must be absent from the ranch. It would be nearly a week before his return from the cattledrive. If his suspicions regarding Kirk Bannion were correct there would be trouble. The man would strike with the deadly speed and accuracy of a rattlesnake.

Stars twinkled in a moonless sky; a coyote's yipping call floated up from the canyon floor below. Breck shook off his gloomy speculations. The faint gleam breaking through the black night would be the Gorman ranch-house.

He rode around to the front of the house and rapped on the door without dismounting. It was his first visit to the G Bar G ranch and it was in his mind that the Gorman brothers had not done much with the start given them by old Breck Allen. The tumbled-down buildings, the sagging corral gate, hinted of shiftless ways not to be entirely excused by the depredations of cattle thieves.

A woman's voice came to him.

"Who's that knockin'?"

Breck gave her his name.

"Bill ain't home," informed the voice.

"Open the door," suggested Breck. "It's important."

The door opened reluctantly, revealed a thin, youngish woman in an untidy print dress. She peered at him with frightened, sullen eyes.

"What do you want with Bill, mister? He ain't home. He went over to your place yesterday and ain't come back yet."

"I didn't know Bill was married," smiled Breck. His gaze raked the lamp-lit room behind the woman's angular figure.

"He ain't," said the woman. "I'm Ned's wife—"

"Ned was over at my place with Bill, yesterday evening," continued Breck.

"Ned ain't back, either," interrupted the woman nervously. "Ain't seen 'em since they left yesterday." She eyed him with frank suspicion. "You ride on your way, mister. Mebbe you're Breck Allen—like you say—an' mebbe you ain't. Ned told me to be careful about folks. How do I know you ain't from the Pot Holes on another job of killin'?"

Breck stared thoughtfully at a battered black sombrero on the table near the lamp. He had seen that same sombrero the night before—on Ned Gorman's head. He remembered the band of rattlesnake skin.

"Sorry, mister." There was panic in the woman's voice, as if she sensed what drew his eyes so intently to the table behind her. "I reckon you'd best ride on to Bowie Smith's Lazy S if you want a place to stop tonight. If you're Breck Allen, Bowie Smith'll know it for a fact. I don't." She started to close the door.

Breck spoke sharply. "Leave that door open. I'm talking some more to you."

She obeyed. Terror was in the look she gave him.

"Don't you know Bowie Smith is dead?"

She shook her head. "No—I wasn't hearin' he's dead—" She gasped the words.

"You don't know that Pete and Denny are lying dead, at the round-up camp down the creek?"

"I ain't heard nothin'," insisted the woman sullenly.

"It's mighty strange you haven't heard about Bowie, Mrs. Gorman." Breck spoke quietly. "That's Ned's hat—there on the table, which proves he's been back since he was over at the Circle B last night. He knew about Bowie Smith—promised to tell Denny and Pete about the killing."

"I—I don't know nothin'!" she repeated faintly.

Breck swung from saddle and was suddenly inside the room.

"What is wrong here, Mrs. Gorman? Why are you lying to me?"

"I'm scared," she faltered. "All these killin's—" Her mouth quivered. "Gawd! I wish I'd never seen Ned Gorman!" Work-worn fingers clutched the soiled print dress. "I—I hate this damn country!"

"Sit down, Mrs. Gorman." Breck spoke gently. He studied her with pitying, worried eyes. "Why is Ned hiding from me? Don't tell me again that your husband is not here."

The woman sank down on a chair. "Ned ain't hidin', Mr. Allen. He's been hurt—" Her gaze wavered toward the bedroom door.

Breck drew his gun. "I'll take a look at him," he said grimly. "I'm a good doctor—sometimes—" He flung the door open. "Come out of there, Ned. I want to talk to you—"

"I'm layin' here on the bed, Breck." The man's tone was sullen. "That onery bronc of mine got to pitchin' and shore throwed me good." There was a groan from the dark room. "Busted my shoulder an' a couple of ribs—"

Breck looked at Mrs. Gorman. "I want a light." He motioned at the lamp. "Take it into the bedroom."

The woman obeyed. Her hands were shaking. Breck waited, drawn to one side from the open doorway. From where he crouched, gun in hand, he got a glimpse of the now lighted room. Mrs. Gorman placed the lamp on a table and backed away with a frightened look at the man lying on the bed under a blanket. A pain-twisted grin contorted his sunburned, unshaven face.

"It's the way Letty told yuh, Breck," he

confirmed. "With me layin' here and not able to handle my gun, we wasn't wantin' visitors tonight—not 'til Bill gets back. Never can tell what kind o' skunk in yore yard these times." He stifled a groan. "Poor old Bowie . . . shore would like to know who laid for him out there in the chaparral."

Breck withdrew hand from holstered gun and framed himself in the doorway.

"Sorry you got busted up, Ned," he sympathized. "Where's Bill? Thought you two were going to carry the news to Pete and Denny."

"Why—it's like this," hesitated the man under the blanket. "Bill figgered there was no sense both of us goin' to the Lazy S, so he went on to Calico to see that lawyer shark o' Val Stamper's." Ned Gorman scowled, stifled another groan. "We got a note due at the bank and Bill figgered he might talk Bannion into givin' us another year on the damn thing." The junior partner of the G Bar G smiled wanly at the tall young man in the doorway. "We're bankin' on you, Breck. We'll shore soon have these rustlers dancin' on air—now you're back in the Calico country."

"You say Bill rode on to town," gently prodded Breck. "He left it to you to tell Pete and Denny about Bowie—"

"That was the idee." Ned Gorman's tone was rueful. "Only trouble about it was that hunk o' sin I use for a horse, got to pitchin' and landed me on them boulders in Calico Crossin'." He forced another pain-contorted grin. "Busted a shoulder and a couple of ribs. Was all I could do to climb back into the saddle and stick there 'til I got home."

"I'll take a look at you," Breck offered. "I know a few things about broken bones. Was two years with the Texas Rangers while I was gone from here."

"No call to do that, feller," protested Ned Gorman quickly. "Letty shore fixed me up good as any doc could do. Means layin' here for a spell, which is some tough on old Bill—what with fall roundup due next month."

"So you didn't get to Pete and Denny with the news about Bowie," ruminated Breck.

"Figger it for yoreself," grumbled Ned Gorman. "No chance for me to ride over to the Lazy S—the fix I was in."

"You wouldn't know about Pete and Denny?"

"I know now," muttered the G Bar G man. "Heard yuh tellin' Letty." His voice hardened. "My God, Breck! It's up to you to work fast—else there won't be none of us left. No tellin' who's next on the list. That's why Letty was scared to open the door to yuh. She figgered them wolves had come to get me—or Bill—or both of us."

A corner of the blanket fell away, revealed a blood-stained bandage. Breck's eyes narrowed.

"You've been bleeding, Ned," he said softly.

"Was cut some—when I hit them rocks in Calico Crossing," explained the rancher.

"I'll have a look at those cuts," Breck told him.

"You leave 'em alone!" Gorman's tone was surly. "Letty's fixed 'em."

Breck smiled at the woman. She was ghastly pale, her eyes big with fright.

"Did you probe for the bullet, ma'am?" he asked gently.

Mrs. Gorman shook her head. "It went clean through," she muttered.

An oath exploded from the man under the blanket.

"Keep yore mouth shut!" he yelled.

There was a scream from his wife.

"Look out! He's got a gun—"

Gorman's left hand whipped from under the cover. Flame spurted—the little room rocked to the crash of the .45 clenched in his fingers. Breck staggered against the wall, slid his length to the floor.

"You've killed him!" moaned the woman.

Her husband flung off the blanket and sprang from the bed. He was fully dressed and carried his right arm in a sling.

"If he ain't dead, I've another bullet for him." The rancher swore. He glanced down at the sprawled form of the Circle B man. "Reckon I'll make certain he's dead—" The gun dangling in left hand swung up.

"No!" screamed his wife.

She flung herself like a wildcat on his lifting arm. A second explosion rocked the room. The smoking gun thudded on the floor from Gorman's nerveless fingers. He swayed drunkenly, a silly look of surprise on his unshaven face, then suddenly the flame of life in him flickered out. He went down like a stricken tree, lay inert at the woman's feet.

She leaned away, arms stretched wide against the wall at her back. There was no pity in her wide, staring eyes. Only horror and loathing.

Her gaze went slowly round to Breck, and after a moment she bent down and looked intently into his face. He was breathing. He was not dead.

Letty straightened up with a little cry. Ned Gorman's bullet had merely glanced across Breck's skull and barely grazed the scalp. The shock had knocked him senseless.

She ran from the smoke-filled room and was soon back with a pan of water and a towel.

Breck's eyes opened, stared dazedly at the woman down on her knees by his side and dabbing a wet cloth on his head and face. She gave him a relieved smile.

"You're awful lucky, mister," she said composedly.

Breck got to his feet unsteadily and stared at the dead man on the floor.

"He was fixin' to plug you again," explained Letty. She faltered. "I—I grabbed his arm . . . the gun went off—"

The Circle B man nodded. "You saved my life, Mrs. Gorman," he told her soberly. "You're a brave woman."

"I—I can't stand it in this room," she gasped. "I don't want to see him again—never. . . . I hate him!" She ran out with a choking cry.

Breck followed her into the front room.

"Sit down," he said gently.

"I want to get away from this house!"

Sobs tore at her throat, shudders racked her thin body.

Breck pressed her into a chair.

"I'll get you away," he promised. "Don't you worry, Mrs. Gorman."

She dabbed at her wet eyes.

"Listen, Mr. Allen. . . . They—they're goin' to lay for your trail herd in Shoshone Pass—"

Breck took the news quietly. To learn that the Gorman brothers were members of the rustler gang, saddened rather than surprised him.

"How long has this been going on?" he questioned her.

"More than a year, I reckon," Letty answered. "Maybe longer. Bill and Ned were mighty secret about their cow-stealin'. I never would have known only for Bill gettin' shot up. Some fellers toted him home and let it out they'd been on a raid." She shuddered. "I was scared to death. Bill and Ned said they'd kill me if I didn't keep my mouth shut."

"You've had a tough time," sympathized Breck. He shook his head sorrowfully. "Bill and Ned were decent boys in the old days . . . used to work for my dad. He helped set 'em up in the cattle business."

"Sure, he did." Letty shrugged her thin shoulders. "It was when I married Ned. I thought he was a decent feller. He turned into a wolf—and Bill, too."

"Would you know any of the gang?" queried Breck.

"None of 'em ever was here, save that time those fellers toted Bill home."

"Were they all strangers?"

"There was one feller I knew—" Letty hesitated. "He'd kill me if he ever gets to know I told on him."

"Don't you worry." Breck's tone was grim. "He won't live long enough."

"I reckon you know him," Letty said reluctantly. "Fish Tay of the Box T—"

"I'm not surprised," Breck assured her. "Fish Tay's a no-'count *hombre* and always has been. Won't be long before he's swinging from the end of a rope."

"I can tell you a lot more," the girl said in a low tone.

"I'm listening—"

"It was Ned and Bill killed Bowie Smith. Bowie found out they were mixed up with the rustlers. They knew he would tell you, so they laid for him in the chaparral."

"And they killed Pete and Denny—on their way back from my place—last night?"

She nodded miserably.

"Rustled Bowie Smith's herd, too. Ned got a bullet in his shoulder." Letty eyed him curiously. "What made you ask me about the bullet, Mr. Allen?"

"Too much blood for a broken bone," explained Breck. "I saw those rags under the bed—blood-stained."

"He bled like a stuck hog," Letty said.

"I'm going to ask you a question—" Breck's face was pale. "You must answer me."

"If anythin' I know will put a rope round Bill Gorman's neck, you can bet I'll answer." Her teeth clicked viciously.

"Did Bill—or Ned—kill my father?"

Letty shook her head. "They knew who done it, though," she declared. "I heard 'em talkin' about it."

"Have you any idea who's the boss of this rustler gang?" he asked.

"I've heard 'em talk of some feller who'd plan the raids." Letty shook her head again. "No, Mr. Allen. I wouldn't know who the feller is.

Never heard 'em call him anythin' but the boss—"

"Val Stamper?" conjectured Breck. He watched her intently. "Didn't you ever hear them talk of *him,* Mrs. Gorman?"

"Sure." She smiled wanly. "They hated him worse'n a skunk—the names they'd call him. No, Mr. Allen—it wouldn't be Val Stamper who's boss of the gang. He's a mean old buzzard, but he ain't mixed up in this dirty business."

Breck stared thoughtfully at the two holes in his hat, made by Ned Gorman's bullet.

"Ever hear them speak of Kirk Bannion?" he asked.

"The lawyer?" Letty shook her head. "Heard 'em cussin' him out to Bowie Smith once— the day Bowie got his notice the bank was foreclosin' his mortgage."

"Ned was saying that Bill was riding into town to have a talk about a note that was due," he reminded the girl.

"Ned was lying," she declared. "Bill brought Ned home after he was shot—when they killed Pete and Denny. They'd had word to join up with the rustler gang for the raid on your trail herd. Ned was shot too bad for the ride and Bill went off alone. Hadn't been gone more'n a couple of hours when you rapped on the door." Anxiety looked from her eyes. "What do you reckon you'll do, Mr. Allen? From what Bill said, the rustlers figure to stampede your cattle into the Pot Holes country."

He regarded her thoughtfully. "Can you find your way to the Circle B?" he wanted to know. "I can ride with you as far as Cat Canyon."

Letty announced she was willing to do anything that would take her a long way from the G Bar G.

"Get ready for the ride," Breck told her. "I'll saddle a horse."

"The red mare," Letty instructed. "She's mine . . . has cat's eyes for the dark."

She joined him in the corral, after a brief interval, the print dress replaced by faded blue overalls, pulled over boots.

"Now, listen," Breck said as they rode out of the yard. "I have a friend, Jane Tallant, staying with her aunt at the ranch. I don't want them to know about this raid on the trail herd. Only worry them for no purpose."

"Sure," agreed the girl. "I'll keep mum—"

"Get hold of Johnny Wing and Dusty Rodes . . . tell them to get word to Sheriff Sorrel in Calico—and to all the ranchers we know we can trust. Tell them I said for the posses to ride hell-bent-for-election to Shoshone Pass."

Letty promised to deliver the message.

"Tell Johnny and Dusty I said it's round-up day for rustlers—and to bring plenty rope," finished Breck. He stared grimly into the black night.

Chapter Thirteen

Indian Flats

Jim Hawker reined his tall red roan in the shallows of Shoshone Creek and meditatively made a cigarette while the horse slaked thirst.

Behind him lifted the dust of the trail herd surging up from the canyon and pouring in a long clamorous line from funnel-like cliffs into the mesa known as Indian Flats.

The setting sun splashing the Panamints with crimson and gold, lay yellow on the mesa. Already the shadows of eventide were creeping up the slopes, darkening the hollows and deeps of gorge and canyon with lavender and blue.

Smoky Peters and Larry O'Day splashed their horses into the stream and promptly reached for tobacco and cigarette papers.

Smoky gazed longingly at the wind-riffled water.

"No foolin'!" he declared. "Here's one cow-poke who goes swimmin', come sundown."

"Make it *two*, feller," grinned Larry. "I've shore gathered enough dust to make a swamp of this creek—time I get washed all clean."

The grizzled foreman smiled at them tolerantly. "Why don't yuh go find yore swimmin' hole now?" he suggested. "You two boys will do first trick ridin' herd after supper."

"Don't look for any trouble with the critters tonight," observed Larry O'Day. "All that bunch o' beef craves is water and grass, and there's plenty of the same to keep 'em restin' easy."

Jim Hawker, veteran of the long trail, shook his head. "Trouble comes when yuh ain't lookin' for trouble," he said dryly. "No tellin' what will happen on a drive. I'd shore hate a stampede up on these flats. We'd be days combin' the Pot Holes and lucky to round up half of 'em."

His keen old eyes probed the rugged slopes below as he spoke.

"Thought I saw something movin', down there in that gully," he added uneasily. He gestured. "Down there—in that clump of madrones—"

"A rider!" exclaimed Smoky Peters. "Headin' away from here—down the arroyo."

"*Two* riders," amended Larry.

They reined their horses up the bank and stared silently until the distant riders dipped from view in the fast deepening darkness of the gorge.

The spear-head of the herd bellowed up, frantic for the water, ploughed belly-deep into the stream. Jim Hawker jerked a nod at the two cowboys. "Go get yore swim. There's a good hole round the bend—under the falls."

"We've been there before," grinned Smoky

Peters. He jogged away, upstream, followed by his companion. The foreman swung the red roan across the mesa toward the chuck-wagon. His expression was grave. The safety of the trail herd weighed on his mind. The glimpse of the two strange horsemen in the gloomy gorge left him apprehensive. Ordinarily he would not have worried. But these were not ordinary times. The growing boldness of the rustlers was a grim reality. The thousand prime beef steers in the Circle B trail herd made a tempting prize for the mysterious raiders of the Calico country.

Pleasant smells of frying steaks and hot coffee greeted the foreman as he rode up to the camp. He climbed wearily from his saddle and turned the roan horse over to the wrangler. The cook grinned round at him.

"Hi, Jim!"

Hawker lowered himself down on a box. "Need any help, Limpy?" He eyed the scant woodpile. "You'd better get one of the boys to drag up some wood for yuh."

Limpy eyed him shrewdly. "What's on yore mind, Jim? What's worryin' you, old timer?"

"Old age, I reckon," grunted the foreman. He forced a wintry smile. "A cup of yore hot coffee'll fix me up."

The cook filled a big tin cup from the coffee pot. "You ain't foolin' me, Jim," he challenged. "I know what gives yuh that long face." Limpy poked the red coals of his fire. "You got rustlers on yore mind."

"Bad place, here on the flats—for a stampede," Hawker said.

"There!" crowed Limpy. "I knowed yuh had rustlers on yore mind." He scowled, glanced at the rifle that leaned against the tail-board of the chuck-wagon. "Won't be the first time I used that old Sharps on rustlers, Jim." The cook grew reminiscent. "Remember that time down on the Chowchilla—when the Sontag gang jumped us—"

Thundering hoofs interrupted Limpy, a jeering voice.

"We've heard that story a hundred times, Limpy! Ain't yuh figgered a yarn that don't rattle old bones?"

The cook's indignant gaze swung to the four dust-grimed riders grinning from their saddles and fastened on the speaker, a short, bow-legged, swarthy man.

"Yore talk don't listen good to me, Pecos," he said severely. "I'm makin' yuh pay an' sweat for them disrespectful words." He gestured at the too-small woodpile. "You don't eat 'til yuh drag me some of them bull-pine logs from yonder." He gestured again. "Git a move on yuh, Pecos— if yuh crave steak and coffee—"

The grin left the swart cowboy's lean face. "I ain't no cook's swamper," he sneered. "Go an' git yore own firewood, Limpy." He stepped down from his saddle.

"Feller,"—Jim Hawker's tone was curt—"climb back in yore saddle and go for that wood. Yore fault you get the chore—talkin' to the cook out of turn like yuh done."

Pecos hesitated, scowled, flung up to his saddle with a muttered curse and rode away. The cook raked the puncher's subdued companions with a triumphant glare.

"Grub's ready," he announced crisply. "Come an' git it!"

The bawlings of the herd faded with the twilight as the leg-weary cattle spread over the mesa. Thirsts quenched, they fed contentedly from the plentiful summer-cured grass. Stars broke through the dark bowl of the sky, twinkled diamond points in the black void of the night.

The murmur of sleepy voices lifted above the crackle of the campfire, kept in blaze by the lord of the chuck-wagon. Anxious lines grooved the veteran cook's face as he peered into the inky blackness beyond the zone of firelight. Across his knees rested the big Sharps buffalo gun and a long-barreled six-gun was in the holster now buckled over lean hips.

He threw an impatient glance in the direction of the drowsy voices.

"You cowpokes better git yore sleep," he

grumbled. "Come ten o'clock an' it's yore turn to fork saddle an' do night herd."

One of the voices told Limpy in impolite words of a certain hot place the cook could make his abode for all the speaker cared.

"I won't forgit them words, Salty," promised the boss of the chuck-wagon grimly.

Snorts came from the unfortunate Salty's two companions.

"No molasses on *yore* flapjacks in the mornin'," jibed a sleepy voice.

Silence fell over the camp, broken only by gentle snores, the crackle of the fire. The cook continued his vigilant probe into the darkness. From the distance drifted the voice of a herd rider lifted in a plaintive cowboy song.

Jim Hawker pushed in through the night's black curtain and spoke curt words that brought the snoring Circle B men scrambling to their feet.

"Fork yore saddles," he said grimly. "Plenty trouble on the prod—"

There was a hasty buckling on of gun-belts, a rush for horses.

"Larry an' Smoky ain't been seen since they rode up the creek to the falls. I've hunted all over the flats for 'em." The old foreman's voice was panicky. "Limpy, something's happened to them boys!"

"Mebbe they've sloped on yuh," suggested the cook, "or went an' got drowned or somethin'—"

"That's fool talk," reproved Jim Hawker. "Smoky an' Larry ain't the breed to run away— an' they ain't got themselves drowned. No sign of them at the swimmin' hole under the falls. There's something awful wrong, Limpy."

"Pecos never come back with that wood," reminded the cook. "Seen Pecos anywheres, Jim?"

The foreman shook his head. "He's gone, too."

"Only one answer," muttered the cook. "It's rustlers, Jim—"

A rifle roared in the distance, reverberated in diminishing echoes from canyon walls. The night-herd rider's song ended in a shrill yell and the men grouped at the campfire saw what was apparently a ball of leaping flames roll across the flats from the mouth of a ravine. A sudden rumble shook the ground under their feet as a thousand terrified steers rose from their rest and stampeded blindly into the black night.

A rifle bullet screamed into the campfire, sent red sparks showering over the cook. He sprang aside with a furious oath and ran for his horse. In a moment, the foreman and the three cowboys spurred into the concealing darkness.

The thunder of the stampede drew an agonized groan from the veteran trail boss. He knew what had happened. There was no mystery for him in that rolling ball of fire. The rustlers had bound a bundle of inflammable brush on the back of a luckless horse and sent the maddened animal—a living torch—straight for the sleeping trail herd.

His rifle spurted fire; the ball of flame abruptly ceased its wild flight across the mesa.

The foreman lowered his gun and looked with grim eyes at his four companions.

"Salty," he said quietly, "you back-trail to the ranch. Mebbe yuh'll run into Breck . . . he should have been here at sundown. If yuh don't meet him, keep goin'—get word to Clem Sorrel—"

The cowboy jerked a curt nod, spurred away.

Shrill yells, the crash of six-guns, drove at their ears. Jim Hawker drew his .45 and fired two quick shots, spaced a count of three and sent another red flash into the night.

Three gun-flashes answered the signal, from which the foreman knew that three out of the four Circle B men riding night herd were alive. There was no answering flash from the singing cowboy. The foreman knew that Shorty Jensen would never again lift his voice in song.

The cook dolefully voiced the same thought.

"That first shot got Shorty," he muttered. "Won't sing about that gal in ol' Cheyenne no more, Shorty won't—"

"Flash yore gun, Curly," ordered the foreman. "One shot . . . so the boys can know we're waitin'—"

Curly's six-gun spat a red streak. Answering shots flamed from three converging points, and above the deep thunder of the vanishing herd came the sharp rataplan of hoofs.

The three Circle B riders drew rein, faces tense and hard under the cold starlight.

"There's seven of us," counted Jim Hawker.

"Double that count, Jim," broke in a furious voice. "Circle B is good for any two mangy rustlers—"

"Make the count anyway yuh want," snarled another voice. "I'm good for five of these skulkin' wolves any time . . . day or night—"

"I was takin' skelps afore you rannihans was born," rasped the cook. He reined his horse close to Jim Hawker's tall red roan, the big Sharps rifle in the crook of his arm. "I'm shore takin' some more skelps tonight!" he yelped. "Injuns or rustlers —a skelp's a skelp!"

"Where's Pecos?" another voice harshly wanted to know.

"Where's Larry—an' Smoky?" demanded a second rider worriedly. "Why ain't them cow-pokes showin' their faces?"

"We know why Shorty Jensen ain't here," muttered a third voice gloomily. The cowboy swore feelingly. "Let's go!" he exploded. "I aim to git me a rustler's skelp—"

Jim Hawker's gaze swept the circle of faces showing grim and hard under the starlight. He knew the metal of these Circle B riders— tempered steel, forged in the bitter wars of this far-flung range.

His hand lifted in a fierce gesture.

"Listen!" he said.

Already the thundering beat of stampeding hooves was dwindling in the distance, fading in the deeps below the mesa.

The cowboy who was Shorty Jensen's friend swore again.

"We'll follow 'em to hell!" he choked.

They all knew he meant the Pot Holes, lying directly below the mesa, that vast maze of canyons reaching down the east slope of the Cactuses to the desert.

Still the Circle B foreman hesitated.

"One of us must wait here," he told the others. "Breck figgered he'd catch up with us—"

"It don't look good—Breck not gittin' here," muttered the cook uneasily.

"They got him," gloomed another voice. "They got Breck like they got Larry—an' Smoky—"

The foreman flung a hard look at the last speaker.

"Mebbe they got Pecos, too," he said softly.

"Mebbe so." The cowboy's tone was skeptical. "Never did trust that feller," he added darkly.

The faint crackle of six-guns reached up from the brush-clad slopes below. The foreman's red roan squealed under the bite of spurs and fled into the black night. The others strung out behind the roan's tall rider—canyon walls flung back the rataplan of drumming hoofs.

Chapter Fourteen

The Devil's Bowl

It was close on midnight when Breck reached the wide sandy wash of the Arroyo Honda and reined the tired gray horse in a clump of concealing willows.

It was years since he had been in this border country of the Pot Holes. In the old days there had been a trail following the climb of Shoshone Canyon to Indian Flats where it intersected the main trail below Shoshone Pass.

He gazed up thoughtfully at the rugged slope, bulking black and sinister under the starlight. Somewhere in that maze of canyons lurked the rustlers, prowling wolves on the trail of the Circle B herd.

He rode on slowly, eyes alert for nearly-forgotten landmarks. The numerous cloudbursts of this semi-desert region had a way of changing the topography. He should have no difficulty in finding the old trail. Shoshone Canyon Creek emptied into the Arroyo Honda, soon to vanish under the thirsty sands to deep subterranean channels. It was only in the rainy season that the Honda was temporarily swollen with storm waters.

The stallion broke into a fast running-walk. Breck knew the gray horse smelled water. The air came damp and cool from the marsh at the mouth of the canyon. Starlight glimmered in the pool through the tules.

Silver King flung up his head, snorted distrustfully. Breck's hand lowered to gun-butt.

Only deer, slaking thirst. They fled from the tules and disappeared up the brush-clad slopes.

Breck let the stallion drink sparingly. He longed for a cigarette, but resisted the temptation. The flare of a match, the red tip of a cigarette, might easily betray his presence to the enemies he knew were between him and Indian Flats.

The high cliffs drew in closely, shut out the stars. The muted roar of the mountain stream mingled with the creak of saddle leather, the beat of the stallion's shod hoofs. Once, the wild scream of a mountain lion brought a startled snort from the gray horse.

The canyon walls narrowed to a bottle-neck, with the creek taking a five hundred foot plunge into the gorge. Spray lifted in billowing clouds of mist, and suddenly they were through the bottle-neck and in a clearing under the starlight.

Breck drew the horse to a standstill. It was a sinister place, a sort of devil's bowl encircled by sheer cliffs. Huge boulders lay in tumbled heaps, with here and there the harsh outline of a giant cactus starkly etched against the starlight.

Warning was in the stallion's up-flung head, the nervously twitching ears. Breck swung quickly into the deeper gloom of a great boulder.

He could hear no sound, save the thunder of the falls outside the bottle-neck opening into the clearing. A second waterfall boomed in the upper canyon. Breck saw that the stream followed the half-moon curve of the cliffs, racing swiftly to the thunderous plunge down the bottle-neck.

He slid from the saddle and crawled stealthily around the boulder.

Gradually his ears grew accustomed to the roar of the two falls, began to absorb lesser sounds. The stamp of a shod hoof came to him, the drag of a rope in the brush.

He continued to patiently probe the darkness with eyes and ears. Something stirred, a match flamed, briefly revealing a man's face.

Breck waited, watching the red glow of the cigarette. The smoker was sitting on a boulder, a rifle across his knees. A lookout, guarding the rustler gang's trail.

A voice broke the monotonous thunder of the falls.

"I always did figger yuh was a low-down, mangy coyote, Pecos—"

Breck stiffened. Smoky Peters' voice! And Smoky was obviously reviling the guard whom he called by the name of Pecos.

Breck's expression was grim. He knew a Circle B rider who went by the name of Pecos.

Another voice came through the darkness—Larry O'Day's Texas drawl.

"I'm backin' Smoky's statement, feller. I'd make it some stronger, though, an' say yuh're a poisonous sidewinder—"

"Don't worry me, none, what you fool cowpokes think," sneered a thin, hard voice.

The hair on the back of Breck's neck bristled. The speaker was Pecos Slade—a Circle B man.

"If I'd had good sense I'd have filled yuh both with lead when yuh was in that swimmin' hole—"

"You didn't want Jim Hawker to find us layin' dead so close to camp," Smoky Peters retorted.

"That wasn't his *real* reason—" Larry O'Day's voice dripped contempt. "He was afraid to pull off any gunplay near the camp. Don't yuh savvy, Smoky? The shootin' would have spilled the beans for these onery rustlers Pecos has throwed in with."

The renegade Circle B man laughed jeeringly.

"You're a smart *hombre*, Larry, only yuh ain't got it *all* figgered. I pulled off this play to make it look bad for you two *hombres*. Jim Hawker will figger yuh've run off—joined up with the rustlers." The thin, hard voice was a vicious snarl. "I always did crave to git you two fellers. I reckon I've got my wish."

Breck was creeping toward the speaker, hugging the shadows. He heard Smoky's voice, steady, unafraid.

"You ain't got us yet, Pecos."

"You bet he ain't," drawled Larry O'Day. "We'll live to see yuh dance on air, Pecos."

The renegade jeered. "I figger different," he told his prisoners. "The play's about done. I'm fillin' yuh both with lead—soon as the stampede gits goin'." There was an evil relish in his voice. "Them steers'll boil down the canyon an' clean through this damn clearin'. You fellers'll be layin' right here. Won't be much left of yuh when that herd stomps over yuh. Reckon the buzzards won't even bother to look for the pieces—"

"You lowdown crawlin' snake," muttered Smoky Peters.

The crash of a rifle rolled down the canyon walls.

Pecos sprang to his feet, stared tensely up the ravine. Smoky started to speak, broke off, amazed gaze fastened on the vague shadow creeping stealthily toward the unsuspecting renegade.

A second shot rattled down the canyon from the flats, and hard on the sharp echoes the men below heard the muffled boom that told them the stampede was on.

Pecos whirled round to his prisoners, hand reaching for holstered gun. A startled oath froze on his lips and slowly the lowered hand lifted with its mate above his head.

Breck prodded the gun fiercely against the man's back.

"Keep 'em up," he warned grimly. He plucked the renegade's gun from holster and tossed it aside. "Quick," he ordered. "Untie them—"

Pecos sullenly obeyed.

The freed cowboys moved swiftly.

"We should leave the snake layin' where he figgered to leave us," gasped Smoky as he jerked on the knots.

"We'll save him for a rope," Breck said briefly. "Tie his mouth up, too, Larry. Don't want him to yell."

"What yuh figger to do with the cuss?" demanded the Texan, deftly thrusting the renegade's bandana into his mouth and pulling hard on the knots.

"Throw him up on that ledge, between those boulders—where he won't be seen—and fork your broncs."

Breck clattered away on the run for his horse. He sprang up to the saddle. Already his agile mind had seized on the one chance to stop the stampede that threatened to ruin the Circle B ranch.

The thunder of the avalanching herd rolled down on them with appalling swiftness. Gunfire lanced the darkness, rifle shots echoed from the cliffs—the shrill, urging yells of the rustlers.

Smoky and Larry spurred up, hastily buckling on gun-belts. Breck outlined his plan briefly. The cowboys chorused delighted approval and swung their horses toward the bottle-neck.

Breck paused to free Pecos Slade's horse and start him down the trail, out of the way of the milling hooves that soon would choke the little amphitheater from wall to wall.

Driving the riderless horse in front of him, he spurred to the bottle-neck where the two cowboys were busy snaking clumps of tinder-dry brush across the narrow gap.

"We've got 'em licked, boss!" gloated Smoky as he dragged up another pile of brush at the end of his rope.

Breck nodded. He was thinking how helpless it would have been, once the herd poured through that narrow exit and on down the trail. The rustlers could have held that bottle-neck against a hundred men, blocked pursuit until the stampeded steers were across the Arroyo Honda and forever lost in the Pot Holes.

"All set, boss!" shouted Larry O'Day, jerking his rope from its load of brush.

Matches flared in their fingers. Red flames licked greedily through the big pile of brush. Breck and the cowboys sprang for their saddles and spurred quickly to stations high above the level of the floor.

The stampede roared down the ravine, flung battering diapason waves of sound against the cliffs. And suddenly the upper portal was spouting a foaming tide of white-faced cattle. They fled across the clearing, horns lowered, tails up, only to be met by the barrier of fire in the narrow pass of the bottle-neck.

Breck saw the lead steer swing to the left and go bellowing along the circling cliffs back toward the upper portal. The line of wild-eyed cattle followed closely and in a few moments were milling round the bowl. Soon they would be a compact herd, too weary and bewildered to continue the mad flight. The stampede was broken.

The exultant yells of the pursuing rustlers changed to startled cries as they glimpsed the blazing brush in the bottle-neck below. Shouts and oaths mingled with the bedlam of sound from the milling herd. The beat of hoofs on the upper trail abruptly hushed.

A rider appeared in the narrow pass at the upper falls, a vague shadow in the starlight.

"Pecos!" Panic, dismay, marked the hoarse shouting voice. "What the hell—"

Flame spurted from a rifle, and with the echoing crash of the gun the rider tumbled from his saddle. Breck heard Smoky Peters' shrill yell.

"There's one rustler won't be needin' a rope!"

Yells and curses came from the upper trail.

The dead rustler's horse fled back through the gap.

"They're all hot and bothered, boss," chuckled Larry O'Day from behind his boulder. "The skunks can't figger what's happened."

Breck went quickly down the slope, keeping to the shadows. He wanted to have a look at the slain desperado. The man's voice had seemed familiar. He had heard it only the night before, in the ranch office, bemoaning the fate of Bowie Smith.

A glance confirmed his suspicion. Bill Gorman had paid for his treachery with his life.

Breck eyed the convulsed features disappointedly. He would have preferred Bill Gorman alive. The man could have told him things he wanted to know.

A rifle bullet whined viciously past his head. He darted back into the shadows. The brief moment there with the leaping brush flames behind had revealed him distinctly to the rustlers. He heard a startled voice.

"Hell! It's Breck Allen—"

Breck glided back to his station higher up the slope. He knew that startled, furious voice. Al Roan—the Horseshoe foreman—Val Stamper's trusted ranch boss. Dismay mingled with the rage that surged through him. Val Stamper was the arch-fiend . . . his was the cunning brain that had spread ruin and death in the Calico country.

Smoky Peters crawled up, dragging his rifle.

"Who's the *hombre*, boss?" There was a grim note in the cowboy's voice.

"Bill Gorman."

"The skunk," muttered Smoky. "We wasn't wrong about him an' Ned. The double-crossin' *hombres* killed Bowie Smith—like we thought." He swore softly. "I'm cravin' to meet up with Ned—if he's with that bunch yonder—"

"You won't meet him," grimly assured Breck. "Ned has paid his account—"

There was no time for more talk. The roar of a heavy rifle blasted the night, flung reverberating echoes from the cliffs.

"Reckon that's Limpy's ol' buffalo gun," muttered the cowboy crouching by Breck's side. "That ol' fightin' cook shore hates a cow-thief."

Shrill yells floated down from the flats—the hammer of hoofs as old Jim Hawker and his half-score fighting-mad Circle B riders hastened to overtake the rustlers.

The Circle B foreman had seen the red streamers of fire across the trail below and suspected Breck's hand. It was possible that the missing cowboys were with Breck. Jim fervently hoped they were. Whatever amazing thing had happened—one fact was outstanding. The stampede was broken, the herd saved.

"It's Jim—an' the outfit—and on the prod!" exulted Smoky Peters.

Larry O'Day slid in from the shadows.

"We got 'em, boss," he grinned contentedly. "Got 'em like rats in a trap—"

His rifle spurted flame, drove back two men trying to force through the narrow gap.

Guns flared on the upper trail, where Jim Hawker and the Circle B men were pouring leaden hail on the luckless outlaws.

Loud yells, curses, lifted above the roar of the falls as the dismayed rustlers ran for cover. They were fairly trapped, caught between the blazing guns of the approaching riders and the deadly rifle fire of Breck and his companions holding the narrow gap. Only one way of possible escape was left them—down the rugged slope below the trail, where a horse could find no footing.

It was round-up night for rustlers.

Chapter Fifteen

Judge Lynch Holds Court

Sheriff Clem Sorrel pushed from the dark portal of Cat Canyon and spurred his jaded claybank horse down the abrupt descent to the dawn-flushed wash of the wide Arroyo Honda.

A half score men rode at the gaunt law-officer's back. There had been no time to enlist the aid of the scattered ranchers. It was sheer luck that Fred Kelly and his Bar K outfit were in town when Breck's laconic message reached him at the hands of Dusty Rodes. Four more men, including his deputy, Andy Hogan, and old Mat Haley, made up the contingent.

Dusty Rodes had demanded that he be sworn in as a member of the hastily-gathered posse, finally admitting that Breck had left implicit orders for himself and Johnny Wing to remain on guard duty at the ranch.

"The boss cain't bawl me out if you swear me in as a deputy, Clem," craftily argued the cowboy. "I got to obey the law an' ride with yuh if you say so."

"You hightail it back to the ranch," the old sheriff had curtly admonished. "You obey Breck's orders, young feller."

"Doggone the luck!" bemoaned Dusty. "I was wantin' a chance to smoke my guns at Bill Gorman. Listen, Clem—"

He gave the dumbfounded law-officer a brief account of the story brought to the ranch by the haggard-faced Letty Gorman.

"Ned was fixin' to blow Breck's brains out and Letty grabbed his gun . . . the bullet took Ned between the eyes. . . ."

The treachery of the Gormans occupied Clem Sorrel's thoughts as he rode down the sandy wash of the Honda through the rose-pink dawn. He wondered dismally how many other supposedly honest cattlemen were secretly members of the mysterious rustler gang. Fisher Tay, of the Box T, would be among the traitors, he reflected. He had long suspected the bearded Fish Tay of lawless activities. Fish was Bart Cordy's brother-in-law, and Bart was Val Stamper's candidate for the office of sheriff at the fall election.

The sheriff scowled as he thought of Val Stamper. The banker's absence was another mystery. Kirk Bannion and Bart Cordy had been riding Clem hard about the puzzling affair, had dared to insinuate the sheriff knew more than he would admit. The saloon man was openly declaring that Breck Allen had murdered Val Stamper—as he had murdered young Tom Stamper seven years earlier.

Fred Kelly's bay horse forged alongside the

high claybank. There was a grim look on the Bar K man's dusty visage.

"Clem," he said, "the boys don't like you being along. I'm the same way about it. It ain't too late for you and yore deputy to head back for Cat Canyon—and town."

"That's kind of you an' the boys, Fred," murmured the sheriff. "Don't you worry about Andy an' me. We done handled plenty bad men since I was sheriff . . . an' put 'em behind the bars—"

"That's what I'm drivin' at," grumbled Fred Kelly. "Won't need bars for these cow-thieves if you and Andy don't horn into the play."

Sheriff Sorrell chuckled. "I savvy how you an' the boys feel," he agreed tolerantly. "Them days have gone, Fred. The Law is in Calico—now."

"It's lynch law this country needs these times," grumbled the cattleman. "No chance to convict a cow-thief as long as Val Stamper is the boss in Calico. You know doggone well that Val hates you—and hates Breck Allen. The court will do what he tells 'em."

The old sheriff's face was bleak. He knew the Bar K man was not exaggerating. Three arrests in six months—and three cow-thieves turned loose by an intimidated jury.

"Mebbe so, Fred," he said wearily. "Just the same, I got to do my part as the sheriff of this county."

"What this county needs is Judge Lynch—and a jury of cattlemen," declared the Bar K man. He scowled. "We don't need yore law ridin' with us, today, Clem."

The old sheriff made no reply. He was staring intently at a big cottonwood tree that grew on the bank of the wash, where Shoshone Creek emptied into the tule swamp. Something dangled there from a limb, something that swung and twisted with the press of the morning wind blowing in from the desert.

The cattleman riding by his side exclaimed softly, spurred his bay horse. Clem Sorrel and his riders surged closely behind.

They drew rein, gazed in silence at the dead man swinging gently at the end of a rope. From the limb of another cottonwood tree in the canyon's mouth dangled another dead rustler.

Clem Sorrel broke the silence.

"Looks like Judge Lynch has already been holdin' court," he said dryly.

There was no answer from the hard-faced men, no pity in their cold eyes.

Sheriff Sorrel turned his claybank horse to the canyon trail.

"Let's ride," he said crisply.

They clattered up the steep canyon trail, the sheriff in the lead. Those behind him could not see the expression on his seamed, weathered face. There was an oddly contented gleam in the keen old eyes, a hint of elation in the grim smile Clem Sorrel wore.

Mat Haley's raspy voice lifted above the thud of hoofs:

"The jasper in the red shirt was Kansas Kile." The wiry little hotel man's tone was peevish. "Never *will* collect that five dollars he was owin' me on his room rent—"

"Kansas was on the Horseshoe payroll," reminded Fred Kelly thinly. "You should collect yore bill from Val Stamper."

One of the cowboys swore fervently. "What do you make of it, boss?" he called out to the Bar K owner. "Doggone queer bus'ness—Kansas Kile doin' a rustler's dance on air."

"The answer ain't hard to guess," sneered another Bar K man. "Kansas had his neck stretched 'cause he's a cow-thief—same as the whole damn Horseshoe outfit."

"Any of you boys know who the other feller was?" questioned Fred Kelly.

"Never heard his name, but I've seen him a lot in Bart Cordy's saloon," informed a cowboy. "Some feller said he was with Fish Tay's Box T outfit."

"Which don't recommend him none," growled Kelly. "Fish Tay should be keepin' him company on the same limb."

The early morning sun threw long golden fingers up the gorge, the roar of the bottle-neck falls drew near. Clem Sorrel reined his horse and lifted a hand for attention.

"Sounds like the herd up there," he muttered.

Faintly the bawling of cattle floated down to them from the mesa a thousand feet above them.

"Shore thing it's the herd," grinned a Bar K rider, "Circle B steers—and on the move through Shoshone Pass."

"Looks like we weren't needed 'round these parts," murmured the sheriff. He was staring intently at something below the trail.

"Another of 'em," exclaimed Mat Haley. He peered over the bluff, at the limp body sprawled in the rocks near the sun-sprayed waters of the creek.

"Hope it ain't some *hombre* that owes you room rent, Mat," chuckled a voice.

They rode on. No time now to care for the dead. Curiosity spurred them. From all the grim signs it seemed that the rustlers had met with disaster at the hands of Breck Allen's fighting riders.

Ashes lifted under the churning hoofs of their horses as they rode through the bottle-neck into the Devil's Bowl.

The Bar K owner reined his horse. Excitement and admiration gleamed in his eyes.

"Not hard to figger what happened here," he told the others. "Brush fire across the bottle-neck stopped the stampede, got the steers to millin' in a circle."

The sheriff jerked a thumb at a limp body sprawled across a flat boulder near the upper gap.

"Been some fightin' here," he grunted.

They rode over to the dead man. His sombrero had been placed over his face. Clem Sorrel leaned from his saddle and lifted the hat for a look.

"Bill Gorman," he muttered. He dropped the hat back on the staring eyes of the dead G Bar G man and shook his head sadly.

"He died too easy," grumbled Fred Kelly. "The double-crossin' varmint had a rope and a tree comin' to him—same as *those* fellows got—" The cattleman pointed up the slope to the forms dangling from the gnarled limb of a scrub oak.

The sheriff's eyes bulged as he stared. There was something familiar about the bulk of one of those hanging dead men.

"Al Roan," said Mat Haley softly. "It's Al Roan—hangin' there from that tree, Clem." The little hotel man's voice went suddenly shrill. "By golly, Breck Allen is shore playin' Judge Lynch to the limit—stringin' up Val Stamper's ranch boss—"

The sheriff eyed him coldly. "We're not speakin' names out loud, Mat. You can think what you like, but it ain't yore business to tell me *what* you think." The old law-officer's hard glance stabbed at the others. "The same goes for you boys, too." He rode on through the upper gap.

Buzzards were wheeling in the blue sky above the Devil's Bowl as the sheriff and his posse left that scene of death.

They pushed up the winding trail, eyes grimly noting other limp bodies sprawled among the boulders on the slope below the trail. And not a man riding behind the sheriff but regretted he had not been among those present when honest cowmen with blazing guns had forever broken the power of the mysterious raiders of the Calico.

The long trail herd was slowly moving across the mesa, winding up the slope to the beetling cliffs of Shoshone Pass. Dust lifted, billowed in a long dull plume across the hills.

Breck and Jim Hawker rode toward the posse emerging up to the flats from the lower trail. The sheriff lifted a hand in greeting.

"How's tricks, son?" His tone was nonchalant. "Gettin' started through the pass kind of late, ain't yuh? Should have had the critters movin' come sun-up."

Breck eyed the old man's placid face a bit doubtfully, took a look at the expressionless faces of the riders behind him.

"Got delayed a bit, Clem," he drawled.

"Don't be afraid to talk, son," the sheriff said

mildly. "You know why I'm here. I got yore message you sent by the Gorman woman."

"We had a brush with the rustlers," Breck admitted. He glanced at Jim Hawker's poker face. "Luck was with us."

"Shore was," grunted the Circle B foreman. "Hot time while it lasted, Clem. Reckon you saw things when you come up the trail—"

Sheriff Sorrel nodded. "Nothin' else you could do but fight—when yore herd was jumped." He shrugged dusty shoulders. "Nothin' else you could do," he repeated emphatically.

"Smart work—that brush fire in the bottle-neck," observed Fred Kelly admiringly.

"Breck was down there, with Smoky an' Larry," explained Jim Hawker briefly. His bitter gaze strayed to a long object covered with a blanket. "Two of our boys was killed," he added in a gruff voice. "That's Larry O'Day—layin' there." He shook his head sorrowfully. "Smoky Peters is all broke up about Larry—"

Pitying glances went to the cowboy sitting on his heels by the side of his slain friend and staring gloomily across the vast panorama of rolling hills.

Breck took the old sheriff to one side.

"You saw things—coming up the canyon," he began. The sheriff interrupted.

"I saw plenty, Breck," he said curtly. "I saw rustlers layin' dead with guns in their hands.

They got what was comin'." He stared for a moment at the crimsoned peaks of the distant Panamints. "You've nothing to worry about, son," he added in a kindly tone. "I saw enough to know you done a good job." He smiled grimly. "I'm thinkin' cow-stealin' has gone out of style in this Calico country, Breck."

"A good half of them were Horseshoe men—Val Stamper's men," Breck said harshly. "The job is not finished until Val Stamper pays the penalty."

"Son"—Clem Sorrel's tone was troubled—"I'm still thinkin' there's somethin' we ain't uncovered about this business—"

"Al Roan was with the bunch . . . we caught him red-handed—"

"Mebbe so," interrupted the sheriff hastily. "Just the same, we ain't convictin' Val on account of Al Roan's doin's. Val's still missin'," he added glumly. "Kirk Bannion an' Bart Cordy are spreadin' round that you've killed him."

"I'm having a talk right soon with Kirk Bannion," promised the young Circle B man fiercely. "I'm riding back now, with Larry and Pete—" He glanced at the blanket-covered forms. "Maybe Fred Kelly will lend me a couple of his boys to help Jim. Smoky'll want to go to the ranch with Larry . . . Leaves Jim short-handed—"

"Take yore pick," grinned the owner of the

Bar K. "A little *real* work won't hurt any of 'em."

"Reckon I'll take Montana—an' Billy Sand," selected Jim Hawker. "Montana an' Billy was workin' for the Circle B long before there was a Bar K outfit in this county."

"You would go an' pick those two rannihans," chuckled Fred Kelly. "Well, shore glad to get rid of the old longhorns for a spell. Talk yore head off if you give 'em a chance. We'll have some peace at the Bar K with them away."

The two veterans glared at him. They were known for their habitual silence.

"No chance to get a word in sideways when *you* horn into a crowd," retorted Montana as he spurred away.

"Well, son,"—the old sheriff's tone was bland—"I'll be ridin' down the canyon with Fred an' the boys. Want to have a look at them rustlers you left layin' around so careless. Mebbe some faces among 'em I've got rewards posted for—"

"You won't find Fish Tay," Breck grumbled. "I wanted Fish Tay . . . always did suspect he knew who killed Tom Stamper."

"Reckon you won't see Fish Tay round these parts no more," prophesied Clem Sorrel. He frowned thoughtfully. "Was Fish with the gang last night?"

Breck shook his head.

"Mebbe we'll pick him up at his Box T Ranch,"

mused the sheriff. "He'll try and make me believe he wasn't mixed up in this bus'ness."

"Letty Gorman claims he is," Breck told him. "She has the goods on Fish Tay . . . enough evidence to have him thrown in jail."

"He's Bart Cordy's brother-in-law," reminded Clem Sorrel. "Bart will go on the rampage—"

"Cordy is in with the gang," Breck declared. "This job won't be finished until that town is rid of Bart Cordy and his bunch of cutthroats."

"Come to think of it," pondered the sheriff, "Fish Tay ain't been seen round town for over a week." His grizzled brows drew down in a thoughtful frown. "That's right . . . haven't seen Fish since Val Stamper disappeared."

Breck looked at him with narrowed eyes. "Clem," he said softly, "I believe you've struck a lead."

"Looks that way," agreed Sorrel. "It's my idee that the feller who runs this gang has had old Val put away . . . mebbe he's held prisoner at Fish Tay's ranch." He settled his long frame in the saddle. "Reckon I'll ride round by the Box T while I got this posse sworn in and see what's doin' at Fish Tay's place. If I can lay my hands on Fish, I'll clap him in jail."

"Don't forget what happened to Ramon," reminded Breck.

"Won't happen again," promised the sheriff grimly.

"He's yellow . . . we can make him talk," Breck said. "Whoever it was killed Ramon will try to close Fish Tay's mouth—" His voice was worried. "Your jail won't be a good place, Clem."

"No other place, I can keep the *hombre*," the sheriff pointed out testily.

"There's the Circle B," Breck told him. "The old 'dobe *cuartel* back of the ranch office will hold him . . . and nobody need know he's been arrested—"

"*Bueno*," chuckled Sorrel. He nodded contentedly. "If we can pick Fish up we'll smuggle the cuss over to yore *cuartel*, Breck. Right smart idee."

He rode away, down the canyon trail, with his posse.

And watching him go, Breck knew the old law-officer's purpose. No dead men would be found swinging at the end of a rope when Sheriff Sorrel finished his job in Shoshone Creek Canyon.

Breck silently blessed the valiant old friend of the Circle B Ranch.

The faithful Smoky Peters was tenderly roping the lifeless form of Larry O'Day to the saddle he would sit no more. Breck's eyes were hard as he helped. Bitterly he regretted he had not used his gun on Pecos Slade, instead of taking him prisoner. He had hoped to force a confession from the renegade Circle B rider. The man had managed to free his hands and make his escape. It was a bullet from Pecos Slade's gun that had snuffed the life from Larry O'Day. No chance now to ever learn anything from Pecos. The sheriff would find his body, lying with other slain rustlers on the rugged slope below the trail. Smoky Peters had exacted swift vengeance for the shot that had killed his buddy.

Breck's gaze went to the high cliffs of Shoshone Pass. The trail herd had vanished into the great gorge. A vast dust cloud hung in the sky. Breck heard faintly the bellowing of resentful steers, the high yip of urging cowboys.

Soberly he rode across the mesa toward the homeward trail, followed by Smoky Peters, leading the two horses with their pitiful burdens.

Chapter Sixteen

The Bearded Rider

Jane did not see her danger until she made the sharp turn in the trail. The brown mare snorted, slid to a halt.

For a moment the girl stared blankly at the big, bearded man on the powerful black horse swung broadside across the narrow trail. With an effort she fought down her panic, strove to keep her voice steady.

"You startled me!"

Something like amusement flickered in the stranger's eyes.

"Sure sorry, ma'am. Wasn't meanin' to give yo' a scare." He spoke with the drawling accent of a Texan.

"Oh—" Jane forced a faint smile. "Then perhaps you will please make room for me to pass—"

The man shook his head. He was something of a giant, and decidedly frightening, with his flaming red shaggy hair and unkempt whiskers. Jane saw with growing dismay that this was no chance meeting.

"Please let me pass," she repeated faintly.

"Sorry, ma'am—" He grinned, and suddenly

the long barrel of a six-gun was resting across the horn of his saddle. "Won't be no trouble, ma'am—if you mind."

She was in for trouble, Jane realized miserably. Her own fault, for disobeying Breck's injunction not to venture out alone.

She had left a note for Aunt Sally, still asleep after hectic hours with Letty Gorman . . . her grim tale of the tragedy on the banks of the Little Calico . . . the news of the raid threatening the Circle B trail herd.

The thought of Breck's peril drove Jane frantic. She had set out for an early-morning ride to Cow Creek Flats, hoping against hope to overtake Breck and warn him. She purposely kept the plan from Johnny Wing. He would have objected; also Della Stamper had arrived the previous afternoon, very unhappy and frightened about her father's mysterious disappearance. Jane was reluctant to take the love-sick Johnny away from Della. The girl needed him. Jane understood why she had come to the ranch. Della yearned for Johnny's comfort.

Her fingers closed desperately over the .32 in her holster. The bearded man shook his head warningly. Her hand fell from the gun.

He nodded. "No sense makin' trouble, ma'am," he drawled.

She stared at him defiantly.

"Who are you?" Jane made herself speak

quietly. "What do you want? I'm in a hurry," she added. "Won't you please let me pass—"

Laughter gleamed in the pale eyes set deep under a red thatch of brow. They were a curious jade color, those small, too-close eyes, and the whites had a pinkish tinge. Jane was reminded of a huge wild boar's head her explorer father had brought home from one of his adventures into the little-known places of the world.

"What do you want?" she repeated, and was shocked at the catch in her voice.

"Why, ma'am . . . I'm wantin' yo' company for a day or two—"

Despite the man's respectful tone, the look in those strange, leering eyes sent a chilling wave over the girl. She flung a desperate glance across her shoulder. The ironic amusement in the bearded man's eyes became vocal. Jane had a glimpse of strong tobacco-stained teeth in a brief yawning of red-whiskered jaws.

"No, ma'am," he chuckled, "no chance for yo' to back-trail. Ain't no room for yore bronc to make the swing—"

"I'll scream—if you don't let me pass," threatened the girl. "I have friends . . . Johnny Wing will kill you—"

The pale jade eyes glinted wickedly. "I reckon not yet, ma'am. Right now I ain't got time to bother with Johnny Wing." His huge freckled hand stroked the butt of the rifle in saddleboot.

"Too bad for Johnny—if he comes round—"

"You know Johnny Wing?"

"Lost plenty to that yeller-haired *hombre*," grinned the black horse's rider. "Johnny's a right smart hand at poker—"

"He's smart with his guns, too," flared the girl. "He—he's not far away . . . he'll hear me scream—"

Mirthless laughter rocked the big man, but Jane saw that the long-barreled six-gun continued its deadly menace. There was no chance to reach for the .32 in her holster . . . drive leaden death at that grinning face.

"Johnny's right smart with his guns—like he is with cards," chuckled the red-haired giant. "I'd sure be nervous if Johnny was close . . . only comfort I have is I know he ain't within five miles of where we're havin' this little talk—"

"Get out of my way!" exploded the girl furiously. She tightened rein, set her slim lithe body tense in stirrups. "I—I'll ride you down—"

"Ma'am"—the man's tone was grim—"I'm warnin' yo' . . . make one move an' yore mare drops in her tracks." His gun lifted from saddle horn. "I'm talkin' turkey an' don't yo' mistake me—"

Jane stared at him with growing dismay. The man would keep his promise, kill the mare if she attempted to force her way past him. Her despairing gaze went to the steep slope below the trail. Only a mountain goat could keep footing down *there.*

He saw the surrender in her eyes, slowly pushed gun into holster.

"I reckon yo're Miss Tallant—"

She nodded, mystified that he knew her name.

"I kind o' figgered yo' was Miss Tallant—"

"I—I don't know you," Jane said faintly. "Why would you be knowing me? . . . What do you want with me?"

"The boss wants you." The man grinned. "Told me to get you . . . been watchin' the ranch-house since before sun-up."

"Your boss?" Jane's bewilderment grew. "Who's your boss?"

"Well, ma'am,"—his tone was impatient—"you can ask the big boss all the questions you've a mind to ask when you see him. I'm takin' you to him now an' yo' won't come to no harm from me—if you don't go makin' me trouble."

Jane studied the black horse. The brand was a Box T . . . Fisher Tay's brand.

Fisher Tay! This unprepossessing stranger was Fisher Tay.

Jane recalled that Breck had spoken of the man. He owned a cattle ranch in the Cactus Hills country. His reputation was bad, from what she had gleaned, listening to Sheriff Sorrel that night at Mat Haley's hotel. Tay was suspected of being over-friendly with rustlers . . . also he was said to be Val Stamper's friend. It was Val Stamper who had sent this man.

Jane was aware of an odd feeling of relief. This encounter had no connection with the dangers that lurked like crawling red flames in the chaparral reaches of the Circle B Ranch—the menace of hidden guns—waiting to flare the hot poison fangs of death at the man she loved.

"I know who you are," she said coolly. "I know the name of the man who sent you to get me—"

"Yo' sure know mo' than I know," sneered the red-bearded man. His voice hardened. "I'm askin' for yo' to come peaceable—"

"I know who you are," repeated the girl. "I know that brand on your horse—Fisher Tay—"

His face darkened.

"Yo're loco!"

For a terrifying moment Jane thought the lifted gun would pour crimson-streaked death at her. The man's voice, gruff, deadly, went on, broke that brief horror. He was reassuring her—and again warning her.

"It's up to yo'self," he finished. "If yo' don't come peaceable, I'll be ropin' them nice-lookin' legs tight an' lash yore hands to the horn of yore saddle." He swung down from his saddle, towered above her, gigantic, terrifying, in the hard white light of the mid-morning sun.

Jane's head went back, with the recoil of her slim body from his huge reaching hands.

"Don't you dare to touch me!" she warned furiously.

The green eyes jeered at her. "I'm ropin' yo' to yore saddle," he said with a crooked smile. "Yo' sure are one spunky she-cat," he added crossly. He undid his lariat with a swift jerk.

Jane's spurs raked the brown mare's flanks. The startled animal snorted, reared—went plunging down the steep slope. The girl felt herself hurtling from the saddle, was dimly aware of a horrified shout from the man—then suddenly all was a merciful blank.

Chapter Seventeen

Where is Jane?

Twilight shadows were lengthening when Breck and Smoky Peters rode into the yard with the lifeless bodies of the two slain Circle B men lashed to the saddles of the led horses.

A frightened old lady met them at the gate.

"Breck! We can't find Jane! She's disappeared—"

He got down from his saddle, stared dumbly at Jane's aunt.

"Johnny and Dusty are looking for her in the chaparral. Della is with them . . . she came out from town last evening . . . hoping you'd have news about Mr. Stamper."

"How long has Jane been gone?" Breck's voice was unsteady.

"All day," Aunt Sally told him. "I found a note, saying she planned to overtake you on the trail. She was so worried when Letty Gorman told us about the rustlers—"

"I'll have Johnny's hide," began Breck furiously.

"It wasn't his fault," defended Aunt Sally. "Jane just slipped away . . . none of us knew what she was up to!"

"He's coming now," interrupted Breck. He

gave the old lady a reassuring look. "Don't worry . . . I won't jump on him. Nobody is to blame. It's just the thought of Jane that drives me crazy."

She clasped his hand, smiled up from wet eyes. "Jane loves you, Breck. She told me last night—"

He tried to speak, could only return the press of her hand. "Don't worry," he said again, huskily. "We—we'll find her—"

Johnny and Della rode into the yard. The young cowboy's face was pale. Della gave Breck an imploring look.

"Johnny is blaming himself," she said, "but it wasn't his fault, Breck—"

"Nobody is to blame . . . I'm not blaming him," reassured the boss of the Circle B a bit gruffly.

Dusty Rodes and Letty Gorman tore up from the creek. Mrs. Gorman flung out of her saddle.

"It's more of that dirty business Ned and Bill were mixed up with," she declared despairingly. "I want to help, Mr. Allen . . . I can use a gun good as a man—"

"Thank you, Letty. You can stay . . . take care of things—with your gun—" Breck spoke gratefully. "We're riding for Calico as soon as we change to fresh horses. I'll leave you in charge of things, Letty."

"You get goin'," Mrs. Gorman said. "I'll be on the job here."

Dusty Rodes's gaze followed her into the patio.

"She's got plenty nerve," he muttered. "She's all right, that girl is. Ned Gorman gave her a tough deal, but he didn't break her." He spurred away to the barn.

Johnny Wing hung back, eyed Breck worriedly.

"What do yuh think happened, boss?" he asked in a low voice. "What's the answer to this business?"

"Kirk Bannion."

Breck's voice had the hard ring of cold steel.

"Kirk Bannion—is the answer—"

The blond cowboy's face was pale under his sunburn. His fingers clamped over gun-butts.

"Let's ride, boss!" he said hoarsely. "I crave to meet this Bannion *hombre*!"

<u>Chapter Eighteen</u>

News from Tonio

They halted midway down the slope above the town, concealed from chance alert eyes in the dense shadows of a clump of junipers.

Lights twinkled at them, but there was a noticeable lack of life stirring in Calico, despite the nearly midnight hour when things were wont to be at their liveliest.

Breck shrewdly guessed the reason for the apparent lifelessness. Many of the more promient roisterers were away on the raid that was to have put more gold coins in their pockets. It was not known yet in their haunts that disaster had befallen the rustlers. In the meantime the little border rendezvous was somnolent, awaiting the return of men who would return nevermore.

Somewhere down there, where lights twinkled from gray shapes that were buildings, Breck believed he would find Jane Tallant. He was aware of an odd certainty that the same forces that had spirited old Val Stamper from the scene of his daily activities were also responsible for the girl's disappearance. If he could solve the mystery of the long-lost Horseshoe

Lode he would have the answer. As he had told Johnny Wing, he believed Kirk Bannion was that answer. Bannion was the mysterious third angle—the unknown seeker of the lost lode. Bannion hoped to either wrest the secret from Val Stamper and Jane, or planned to ruthlessly destroy them as trespassers and rivals for possession of a treasure he coveted.

Breck looked at his three companions, their faces limned in hard lines under the starlight. He could not have found the world over, three men more capable for the dangerous task confronting them down in that apparently dozing little cow-town. There was no discounting the perils ahead. Calico was an enemy town; only vigilance, and their proven ability with their guns, could guard them. Breck was aware that he would be an immediate target for the guns of the rustlers' friends. He was marked for death in that town, and the three Circle B men with him would not be suffered to escape.

Of the three, Dusty Rodes was perhaps the fastest with his guns, but few men could throw lead with the speed and accuracy of Smoky Peters and Johnny Wing.

However there was too much at stake to openly challenge the evil forces Breck knew would arouse to swift action at the sight of himself and his men riding into the street. He dare not risk the safety of Jane Tallant by a show of bravado.

He said as much to his three attentive companions.

"We savvy, boss," Johnny Wing agreed. "Won't do Miss Jane any good for us to be killed right off the bat."

They discussed plans and presently continued down the slope toward the twinkling lights and swung into the dry bed of the arroyo back of the Haley House. Breck vividly recalled the night they had fought their way down that wash, with Jane, to the livery barn. He pulled in the big buckskin he was riding.

"All right, boys," he said to Smoky Peters and Dusty Rodes, "you circle round to Horner's barn and attend to the horses—and don't botch the job."

The two cowboys melted into the darkness. Breck and Johnny dismounted and tied their horses inside a clump of mesquite and made their way stealthily up the bank.

They moved on soundless feet toward the kitchen quarters of the Haley House, vague shadows under the starlight.

The yellow glow of a lamp filtered through the kitchen window. Johnny drifted close alongside and tried to peer into the room. He shook his head, rejoined Breck waiting near the door.

"Wong's feelin' scary," he reported. "He's got the window covered."

Breck tried the door-knob cautiously. The door

was bolted. He rapped gently. The clatter of dishes abruptly ceased and after a brief interval they heard the shuffling movement of the Chinaman's slippered feet.

"Who makee knock on door?"

The cook's voice was frightened. Johnny Wing put his mouth close to the door-jamb.

"It's me . . . Johnny Wing," he whispered. "Open the door, Wong . . . We want to see Mat—"

Another brief pause, then the iron bolt slid back and the muzzle of a .45 appeared in the narrow crack as the door opened slightly. Above the threatening gun-barrel peered a slant eye.

"You know me, Wong," Johnny encouraged. "We want to see Mat Haley—"

Wong muttered something in his own tongue and opened the door wider. The two men slid into the kitchen. The cook closed the door and replaced the bolt.

"What you wantee boss for?" he demanded. He thrust his gun inside baggy trousers and eyed his visitors curiously.

"We don't want it known we're in town," explained Breck. "Tell Mat we want to see him, Wong."

The fat Chinaman nodded and shuffled from the kitchen.

The old hotel man presently joined them, hastily buckling his trousers around his waist, over a flannel nightshirt. Wong came in at his heels and closed the hall door and placidly resumed his dish-washing.

"What's the trouble?" Mat Haley's tone was uneasy. "Clem ain't in town, if it's him you're lookin' for, Breck."

He listened with growing dismay while the Circle B man gave a brief account of Jane's disappearance.

"Clem ain't in town," Mat repeated. "We got in late from Indian Flats . . . come by way of Fish Tay's Box T, like Clem promised yuh he would. Fish wasn't round . . . nobody was there, so we rode on into town. Clem was eatin' supper when a feller brought him word that he'd seen Fish Tay this mornin'—ridin' out of Rattlesnake Canyon near yore place."

Johnny Wing muttered an exclamation, looked at Breck with dismayed eyes.

"That's where we was ridin'—when we lost Miss Jane," he groaned. "Boss, Fish Tay is the *hombre* that got her—"

The hotel man continued his story. "Clem got hold of Fred Kelly an' his Bar K boys and started right out ag'in. Fred an' the boys was still in town . . . stopped to eat supper. Clem was uneasy . . . figgered Fish Tay was up to no good—so close to yore place."

"Thank you, Mat." Breck spoke quietly. "Seen anything of Kirk Bannion?"

"Seen him across the street along toward

dusk . . . goin' into Bart Cordy's place. Kirk don't eat at my hotel," he added. "Seems to like the Spanish food over at Jose Moraga's *cantina*—"

Breck nodded. "We'll go and have a look in the *cantina*," he said briefly. "All right, Mat . . . thanks for the help. Keep it quiet I'm in town—"

"You bet—" Mat opened the door and his two visitors vanished into the night.

In silence they made their way back to the horses down in the arroyo and rode on toward the big livery barn, bulking vague and vast in the darkness.

All was quiet there.

They kept their horses moving at a walk, circled the barn and crossed the street to the other side. Again they pulled to a halt, in the dense blackness of arching cottonwoods that shut out the starlight.

"About time Smoky an' Dusty showed up," muttered the blond cowboy.

The soft thud of hoofs presently reached their straining ears. The two Circle B men drifted toward them from the chaparral beyond the town.

"All fixed," grinned Smoky Peters. "Found the night-man snorin' inside the door an' tied him tighter than a bale of his hay."

"Ain't a bronc left in Horner's stable," gloated Dusty. "Shore will be some peevish *hombres* come mornin'. Say, boss, that was a slick idee—"

"Saw two or three more at the hitch-rail in front of Cordy's saloon," worried Breck.

"We'll get 'em," volunteered Johnny. He slid from his saddle and disappeared into the street, followed by Dusty Rodes.

While they waited, Breck told Smoky Peters what he had learned from Mat Haley. The cowboy listened in grim silence.

"Fish Tay got her," he finally muttered. "Boss, my trigger finger is itchin'—" Smoky's hand tightened over gun-butt, his face bleak under the starlight.

Johnny and Dusty appeared, leading the three cow-ponies left by carousing punchers in front of the Outpost Saloon. They sprang into saddles and continued on into the darkness of the chaparral, driving the confiscated horses in front of them.

In a few minutes they were back and now the four men rode quietly in the direction of Jose Moraga's *posada* at the other end of the town. They passed Cordy's Outpost Saloon, where lights still faintly twinkled. The only other lights they could see shone from the jail, and Sheriff Clem Sorrel's snug cottage up on the hill.

In single file they rode through the black night, working their way quietly through the mesquite trees back of the saloon to the squat adobe building set snugly back in the grove of concealing umbrella trees at the upper end of the street.

They dismounted and went on soundless feet to the front door of the *cantina* and in a moment had slipped into the dimly-lighted room.

It was a long room, with a bar at one end, and tables scattered around on the mud-brick floor.

Breck took in the scene with a swift, sweeping glance. Business was quiet with Jose Moraga. Save for some half dozen swarthy-faced men drinking mescal and playing cards, the place was deserted. There was no sign of Kirk Bannion. There was a chance he might be in one of the several curtained alcoves.

The man behind the bar was eyeing them curiously. He was not Tonio, Breck saw, nor was he fat old Jose Moraga.

With a gesture at the barman that service was wanted, Breck led his men toward one of the curtained alcoves across the room. Curious glances from the card-players followed them.

"Keep your eyes on those Mexicans," Breck warned his companions. "Stop any man who tries to leave."

"You bet," muttered Dusty Rodes. He took a seat close to the curtain, where he could watch the group of card-players.

The barman came in.

"*Buenas noches, Señores*," he greeted politely. "You wish to drink—eat?"

"*Si,*" smiled Breck. "Tortillas—a bottle of wine—"

The barman called out sharply. A young girl suddenly appeared at the barman's elbow, smiling and dimpling at the newcomers. She wore a low-cut bodice and gaily-colored short skirt that showed off trim ankles.

"Attend to them," bade the barman curtly in Spanish. He turned back to his bar, muttering something to the group of men as he passed their table.

Breck guessed the man was reassuring them there was no cause for alarm. He smiled at the waiting girl, fingered a gold piece.

"You are one of Jose's daughters?" he queried.

"*Si, Señor,*" she dimpled.

"*Bueno!*" He held out the gold piece. "I am a friend of Tonio. . . . Tell him that I would talk with him."

The girl took the gold piece. "*Si, Señor.* I will tell Tonio."

She disappeared with a swirl of short skirts.

"Looks like one of them *hombres* aims to leave," muttered Dusty, eyes glued to the crack between the curtains.

"Stop him," ordered Breck curtly.

Dusty and Smoky Peters slid into the main room, guns in hand.

"Keep yore seats," commanded the Circle B's

231

gunman in his chill voice. "No *hombre* leaves till we say so."

There was a sudden hush in the long room, and slowly the Mexican sank down into his chair. Breck spoke from the alcove.

"Take their guns and knives, Smoky. Herd them into one of the alcoves—and that barman with them. I don't trust that fellow behind the bar." He stepped from behind the curtain, guns threatening. "You help Smoky," he told Johnny Wing.

Sullenly the swarthy men and the scowling barman surrendered their assortment of weapons and were herded into an alcove.

Dusty Rodes took a seat at a nearby table, his back to the door, but facing the curtained alcove holding the prisoners. Johnny and Smoky hastily tossed the confiscated weapons out of sight behind the bar and rejoined Breck at their table.

Tonio hurriedly made his appearance from a rear door, paused to look in astonishment around the deserted room, and stare uneasily at the lone *gringo*, apparently dozing at a table near one of the alcoves.

Breck called to him softly.

"*Si!*" muttered the startled half-breed. He glided swiftly across the floor.

"Sorry, Tonio," apologized the tall Circle B man. "Wasn't sure I could trust your crowd. Got 'em stowed away yonder." He jerked a thumb in the direction of the concealed prisoners.

"That is not nice," grumbled the Shoshone. "Jose will be angry—"

Breck interrupted him. "Never mind about old Jose. Here—give him this—to pay for any loss of business." He held out several gold pieces.

Tonio shook his head. "No, *Señor* Breck. I do not want your money. I already owe you my life. I am glad to serve you, *Señor*—"

"I'm looking for Kirk Bannion," Breck went on. "Where is he, Tonio?"

The half-breed shook his head. "I do not know, *Señor*. I only know that he rode away from town—after dark this evening. Miguel, who is my wife's brother, was watching him for me and brought me the news."

Breck's expression was worried. "I'd give a lot to find that man, Tonio," he said fiercely.

The half-breed started to speak, broke off as the girl appeared from the kitchen door with a tray of steaming tortillas. She halted abruptly, gaze roving in amazement around the room.

"*Madre de Dios*!" she exclaimed. "What has happened here?"

Tonio beckoned to her.

"Do not be frightened, Panchita," he cautioned. "This is the *Señor* Breck Allen—my friend. I owe him my life and wish to serve him."

"*Si*, Tonio," whispered the girl. "Carmen has told me the story. I will help, too." She placed the tray on the table and stared with big eyes at the tall young *gringo* who once had saved the life of her sister's husband.

Tonio gestured at the street door. "Throw the bolts and put out the big lamp. We will close . . . receive no more patrons tonight."

Panchita sped away obediently, and Jose Moraga's son-in-law turned shrewd brown eyes on Breck. He was a slim youth, with the high cheek-bones of his Indian forebears. Tonio was clever, with some education.

"*Señor*," he began in a low voice, inaudible to the Mexicans cooped in the alcove beyond, "I have learned much about this *hombre* we call Kirk Bannion. He is what you call a renegade from Sonora, not, as we thought, a *Californio*—"

"Tell me quickly," begged Breck. "Time is short." He motioned to Johnny and Smoky to enjoy the tortillas at which they were looking hungrily.

Tonio beckoned to Panchita as she snuffed the wick of the big lamp. She glided up across the darkened room. He motioned to Dusty, keeping guard on the prisoners.

"A plate for the *vaquero*," he told her.

The girl took one of the loaded plates from the tray and bore it off to the cowboy who gave her a shy, grateful grin. Tonio went on with his story.

"This Kirk Bannion's real name is Esteban Romero—a son of a rich *haciendado* who was ruined by the revolution in Mexico years ago. It is his plan to regain great wealth—start another revolution in Baja California which will spread over all of Mexico. For this he has murdered without scruple. It was he who killed Ramon Matute in the jail, for fear Ramon would tell you the truth—"

"I thought so," nodded Breck.

"He organized this gang of rustlers," continued Tonio. "He has made much money from stolen cows—but not enough—"

"Tonio—" Breck spoke in a husky whisper. "Did he kill my father—"

"I do not know, *Señor*. It is possible." The half-breed frowned. "I fear that he has killed the *Señor* Stamper. He had learned of a great secret possessed by the *Señor* Stamper—something about a lost mine—"

"You have told me enough!" exclaimed the Circle B man. Impatience, fear for the girl he loved, gnawed him. "I must find this man—before it is too late!"

Tonio regarded him worriedly. "It is possible that Bart Cordy will know," he finally said. "They are friends . . . Bart Cordy does his bidding—"

Breck sprang to his feet. The half-breed raised a protesting hand.

"No, *Señor* . . . To go to Cordy's saloon will mean your death. At least a score of his paid gunmen are there—"

"I've got to go!" Breck answered quietly. "It's life—or death—for me to find Kirk Bannion— or whatever you say his real name is."

"I have a better plan," Tonio told him. "I will myself go to the Outpost Saloon—tell Cordy that Kirk Bannion is back—wishes him to come to the *posada* immediately."

Breck considered the idea for a brief moment, then nodded agreement.

"All right, Tonio . . . I'll wait here ten minutes."

"I will bring him in the back way," schemed the Shoshone. "I will tell him Bannion made me close the *posada* early—that he wishes secrecy—" He hurried away, beckoning the girl to follow him.

Breck made his plans swiftly. Bart Cordy would come armed, perhaps bring some of his gunmen with him. The man must be taken unaware—disarmed and made a prisoner before he knew of his danger.

Summoning Smoky Peters and Johnny Wing he stationed them on either side of the kitchen door, through which Cordy would enter. Dusty Rodes must remain at his table, guarding the prisoners in the alcove. Fortunately the room was in semi-gloom and Dusty's back would be to the door. He would look like some lone patron, overcome with mescal and in a drunken sleep.

He went back to his alcove and turned up the lamp. Cordy would naturally believe that Kirk Bannion was in the brightly-lighted booth. He sat down, guns loosened in holsters.

The minutes dragged. Breck could hear the beat of his heart, hammering out the seconds. Suddenly the stamp of approaching booted feet came from the kitchen. The door swung open, revealed the big frame of the saloonkeeper outlined against the lamplight behind him.

For an instant the man hesitated, stared suspiciously at the dimly-seen form apparently slumbering at the table, then as if reassured by the bright light in the alcove he slouched into the room. The door swung shut behind him and again the long room was in deep gloom. A shadowy form was suddenly behind him. Cordy halted as if struck with a paralysis that rooted his feet to the earthen floor. Slowly he lifted his hands above his head as Johnny Wing's gun pressed hard against his spine.

"That's the idee, Bart," approved the cowboy in a grim voice. "You can keep on movin' now—right where yuh was headed for—"

The saloon man obeyed. Out of the corner of his eye he glimpsed another vague shape drifting from the shadows behind him.

Breck eyed him grimly as he halted in front of the lighted alcove.

"Take his guns, Smoky," he said quietly.

The cowboy deftly removed the weapons, one from low-slung holster, another from under the man's coat, a short-barreled derringer. Breck spoke again, his voice low and deadly.

"I'm giving you five seconds to tell me where Kirk Bannion is, Cordy." His gun lifted. "Speak —or I'm sending a bullet between your eyes."

The saloon man's mouth opened, gulped like a fish taken from the water.

"One second left," warned the chill voice.

"Mexican Wells," gasped Cordy.

Breck's hard eyes bored him, probed him mercilessly.

"That the truth, Cordy?"

"I—I swear it!" whispered the ashen-faced saloon man. There was no mistaking the death staring at him from those cold gray eyes. "I'm tellin' yuh the truth, Breck—"

"You're coming with us," Breck said. "All right, boys, let's get moving—"

They marched the prisoner out by way of the front street door, which Tonio unbolted for them. The half-breed had made a sudden appearance from a side door. He motioned for Dusty Rodes to follow the others out.

"I'll take care of these *hombres*," he promised. His white teeth gleamed in the semi-darkness as he closed the big door behind the cowboy and faced round to the scowling faces emerging from the alcove.

"You will be wise . . . make no trouble," he told his angry patrons smoothly. "There is a new law in this town—the law of the *Señor* Breck Allen." He moved toward the bar. "Come—we will cele-brate . . . the house is your host this night. Rubio," he added, "light again the big lamp, and you, Juan Largo—tune up the guitar. We will have music . . . wine and song to celebrate a new day for Calico."

The big lamp's glow flooded the long room. The patrons, their anger forgotten, crowded noisily around the bar. Tonio lifted a hand for silence.

"Listen—my friends—"

From the outside night sounded the beat of horses' hoofs.

Tonio smiled contentedly, lifted his glass.

"To the *Señor* Breck Allen," he pronounced solemnly. "May God go with him—and his business!"

They drank to the dwindling thunder of drumming hoofs.

Chapter Nineteen

Terror at Dawn

Jane had only the vaguest memory of what happened after the fall from the trail. She found herself lying on a bed, a home-made affair that seemed oddly familiar. Her white Stetson hat lay on the floor, dusty, and showing a rust-red stain on the brim. Her hand went to her aching head, touched the wild disorder of her hair. There was a lump—a cut . . . strands of hair were matted with dry blood.

Painfully she got up from the uncovered mattress and stood for a moment, fighting off the giddy feeling that assailed her.

Dawn was streaking the sky, threw pale gray light through the window. Jane stared at the reflection of herself in a dust-grimed mirror. Her face was ghastly in that gray dawn. There was a scratch on her cheek—her flannel shirt was torn, hung in shreds from the smooth roundness of white shoulder. She eyed down at the blue overalls, saw a jagged rock slash running from waist to boot-top. The rowels of one spur were twisted and bent, where her foot had caught in the cleft of the boulder when the mare had lost her footing.

Jane shuddered. Death had been close.

It came back to her—that moment of stark horror when the brown mare went plunging from the trail. She had been thrown from the saddle and held by the projecting stump of a dead madrone tree, saved from following the unfortunate mare down that sheer thousand foot drop to the rocks below.

Saved for what worse fate, Jane wondered miserably.

She moved on unsteady feet to the window. Her legs seemed boneless, bent under her weight like rubber. She clutched desperately at the window-sill, stared out at a dark mass of mountain piling skyward in the dawn's cold gray light.

Those grim ridges lying stark and sinister against a silvering sky had an oddly familiar look.

Jane's gaze went again to the crude, home-made bed. Her eyes widened. She now realized where she was. She had herself carpentered that bed from willow and alder trees.

She went on those strangely bending legs back to the bed, sank down, hands pressed tight over her racing heart.

She was in her own house . . . the log cabin at Mexican Wells.

Dimly she began to understand. This affair had no connection with Breck Allen—the rustlers. Val Stamper was responsible for this abduction . . . Val Stamper—and the long-lost Horseshoe Lode.

Terror poured through her.

The sound of heavy booted feet approaching the door stiffened her courage. It was no time to surrender to weakness.

The door opened, revealed the big red-bearded man.

Jane stood proudly erect, rigid with her indignation. At that moment she would not have hesitated to kill—had her gun been in her holster. The .32 had either fallen from the belt when she had pitched from the saddle, or had been taken by the giant now grinning at her from the doorway.

"What do you want with me?" she asked coolly. "Why have you brought me here?"

He seemed pleased, relieved, by her show of spirit.

"Ain't nothin' wrong with yo'," he said in answer. "Yo' sure took a bad fall when yo' spurred the mare over the cliff. Was scared yo' was dead when I grabbed yo' from that ol' madrone bush—"

"Let me out of this room!" interrupted Jane. "No thanks to you that I'm not lying dead down there in the ravine—with Brown Bess—"

"Yo' sure got plenty temper," chuckled the man. He glanced down at a bucket in his hand. "I figgered yo'd like to tidy yo'self up, ma'am.

That cut on yo' head bled some." He grinned apologetically. "Sorry I ain't got a brush an' comb —an' all the fixin's for a lady—"

"Let me out of this room!" repeated the girl furiously. "I don't want your hospitality—"

He put the pail of water down, pushed it inside the door on the toe of his boot.

"What do you want with me?" Jane flung at him. "What does Val Stamper want—"

There was genuine surprise in the look he gave her.

"Why, ma'am—I ain't workin' for Val Stamper—"

"Yes, you are!" charged the girl hotly. "He thinks I know the secret of the lost mine—"

The red-bearded giant came into the room and closed the door and leaned his big shoulders against it. There was a glint in the pale jade of his eyes that sent a new wave of terror over the girl.

"A lost mine, ma'am? . . . I ain't been hearin' of a lost mine—"

"Do you know the name of this place—where you have brought me?" demanded Jane.

"Sure I do," he answered. "Mexican Wells— in the Cactus Hills country." His tone grew ironic. "Circle B range," he told her.

"Mexican Wells is mine—a homestead," Jane said curtly. "This is *my* house—and I want you to leave immediately."

The man's tobacco-stained teeth glimmered through the thatch of unkempt red whiskers.

"You won't laugh when Breck Allen asks you about this outrage," flared Jane.

He scowled.

"I'm thinkin' Breck won't be round, ma'am—"

Jane stared at him. The heavy beat of her heart seemed to shake the room.

"What do you mean, Fish Tay?" Her voice was a whisper, sharp, sibilant. She cowered back, hands pressed against the mattress. "Why do you say *that?*"

"I ain't answerin' questions," Fisher Tay told her gruffly.

"Why have you brought me here?" Jane persisted. "I—I was thinking—"

"Yo' ain't thinkin' right, ma'am. Val Stamper ain't in this deal—"

"Fish Tay,"—the girl spoke in that same tense whisper, "is this—this man—Kirk Bannion?"

"Kirk never said nothin' of a lost mine," muttered the big man.

"Kirk Bannion!" Jane went rigid. Kirk Bannion. . . . Val Stamper's lawyer.

"What does Kirk Bannion want with me?" she faltered.

His unclean look raked her, made her feel undressed.

"Well, ma'am, a woman with yore face an' yore

figger, don't need to wonder why a man wants yo'."

"You dirty skunk," Jane said contemptuously.

The thick, red-whiskered lips twisted in a crooked smile.

"You was speakin' of a lost mine," he said heavily. "If Kirk Bannion's handin' me the double-cross—it's sure goin' to be too bad for him—an' for yo'self—"

"Get out of this room—or let me out," stormed the girl.

The man's pale eyes blazed at her, let loose a flash of wild passion that brought a startled cry from Jane. Her look went desperately to the window.

"You won't get out through the window," Fish Tay told her in a thickened voice. "I'm tyin them pretty legs to the bedpost."

"Tell me," she pleaded, "is it Kirk Bannion—"

"Yore guess hit plumb centre," growled the red-haired giant. He jerked a buckskin thong from his pocket, moved toward her.

Jane sprang from his reaching hands, threatened the leering face with an uplifted chair.

"Spunky!" He grinned, stood watching her with those inflamed jade eyes. "I like a spunky gal—"

"Don't you touch me!" she gasped.

Sunlight, hot and red from the mountain ridge, streamed through the window, a fiery beam in the cold gray dawn.

Fish Tay hesitated, the leather thong dangling from thick curled fingers.

"You was speakin' of a lost mine," he said again. "I'm askin' yo' to talk fast. What do yo' mean . . . this lost mine—"

Jane reached desperately for the shred of hope offered by the man's aroused curiosity.

"The lost mine . . ." She faltered. "Hasn't Kirk Bannion told you—or Val Stamper—"

He wagged his red head at her.

"Ain't never heard of a lost mine—"

"Then why have you brought me here?"

"Kirk promised me a thousand dollars for me to bring yo' here to Mexican Wells . . . told me he was crazy for yo'—" Fish Tay's voice was venomous. "Looks like Kirk's handin' me the double-cross. I was figgerin' he was wantin' some fun with you—"

"You haven't heard of the lost Horseshoe Lode?"

"Seems like I have," muttered the red-bearded giant. "There's been talk in Calico—"

"I thought you were doing this—for Val Stamper," Jane said, her eyes on the rawhide thong in those thick, curled fingers. "Keep away from me—or you'll be sorry—"

"Sorry!"

Wicked laughter lurked in the pale green eyes.

"I figger it's yo'self will be sorry—if you don't

tell me about this lost mine—this Horseshoe Lode you say Val Stamper's tryin' to find."

"Where is Val Stamper?" asked Jane. She was desperately fighting for time, hoping wildly to distract the man's thoughts. "Why don't you ask him about the lost mine?"

"I'm askin' you," he grumbled.

"I don't know!" insisted the girl.

"I've a mind to shake the truth out of yo'," threatened the man. He moved toward her menacingly.

Jane refused to flinch. She watched him with cold, contemptuous eyes, head lifted proudly. Her coolness seemed to restore his calmness, won a look of reluctant admiration.

"Yo're spunky, all right," he muttered. "All the same, I got to tie yo' to the bed. I promised Kirk I'd keep yo' here till he comes. Ain't takin' a chance on yo' climbin' through the window—" The thud of hoofs jerked him round to the door. He stood in a half crouch, one hand clamped over gun-butt as he listened.

The hoofbeats stopped, they caught the low murmur of voices. Fish Tay's red-bearded face looked round at the white-cheeked girl.

"Reckon that's Kirk Bannion," he said with a relieved grin. "I'm leavin' yo' to Kirk." He jerked the door open. Jane caught a glimpse of the lawyer standing by the side of his horse in the rose glow of the dawn.

For some reason the sight of the man filled her with a sense of horror. Fish Tay was a brutish creature, but Kirk Bannion was a devil. With shocking certainty Jane knew who was responsible for the reign of terror in Calico.

He came in from the quickening sunlight, moving with his noiseless catlike grace and slapping dust from whipcord riding breeches with his gloves. At his sharp word, Fish Tay hurried out to the yard where two men slouched in their saddles. Kirk Bannion closed the door and stood staring at Jane in the bedroom. He smiled.

"It is good of you to meet me here, this morning, Miss Tallant—"

He threw his wide-brimmed hat on the table and pulled out a chair.

"We can talk more comfortably in here," he added with a beckoning gesture.

Jane came out from the bedroom slowly, and slowly sank into the chair.

"What is it you want with me, Mr. Bannion?" she asked quietly.

The lawyer took a chair across the table and carefully made a cigarette, the while eyeing her with absorbed attention.

"I want you to tell me what you know about the lost Horseshoe Lode," he finally answered.

"I do not know where it is, if that is what you mean," Jane said steadily.

"I think you lie." Kirk Bannion's smile was sinister. "Perhaps this will help you remember—" He drew a leather wallet from a pocket and extracted a piece of crumpled, age-yellowed paper. Jane stared at it with mounting interest. She had not seen it before, but knew instantly that it was the crude map described by Jim Hawker as the one found on the dead prospector years before. Jim had seen it in the possession of a desert rat when on a visit to Stovepipe Wells. The mouth of the canyon was roughly drawn in the shape of a horseshoe.

Kirk Bannion's brown eyes were intent on her face, glinted under sleepy lids.

"You have seen it before," he murmured. "You know the secret this old map holds—"

"I have never seen it before," Jane assured him.

"Your expression gave you away." Bannion's tone was curt. "Don't lie to me—"

"I've heard of it," she finally admitted. "If there is a secret there, I don't know and can tell you nothing." She watched him closely. "I—I had an idea that Mr. Stamper possessed this old map," she added.

A scowl passed across the swarthy face opposite her. "I don't mind telling you," Kirk Bannion said softly, "that Val Stamper is dead—"

Jane looked at him with shocked, horrified eyes. "You mean—"

"Yes, I mean that I killed him," continued the purring, deadly voice.

"It—it was your men, then, who tried to murder me in the Painted Canyon—that afternoon—" Jane's voice was a dismayed whisper. The man's frankness shocked her, made her senses reel. This cold-blooded confession could mean only one thing. Kirk Bannion planned her own death.

"The men botched the job," he grumbled callously.

"You—you monster!" whispered the girl. "I—I believe that you killed my father—seven years ago—"

Bannion shook his head. "No, Miss Tallant. Unfortunately for a number of other people, the secret of the lost lode appears to be wrapped up in the mystery of your father's disappearance." His sleepy brown eyes grew agate hard, and violent. "I intend to find the Horseshoe Lode and will destroy any man—or woman—who stands in my way. For a while, old Breck Allen of the Circle B possessed the secret, but didn't know its value. It was one reason why I had to kill him. The other reason was he unfortunately chanced to learn the name of the leader of the rustlers."

"You!" gasped Jane. "You—Kirk Bannion . . . the chief of the rustlers—"

"The Calico country is my empire," he gloated in his smooth voice. "The Horseshoe Ranch, the Circle B, and a half dozen other outfits will be my domain. I'll be the richest, most powerful man in the state when I find the lost lode."

"You are quite mad," declared Jane. "Breck Allen will kill you—kill you like a mad dog."

Bannion scoffed.

"Allen is done for. You won't see Allen again, young woman." He went on with his boasting. "With my vast riches the dream of my life will be realized."

He broke off, stared around, fixed his gaze on a cupboard.

"I have wine cached here," he laughed. "Come—while you make up your mind to tell me the secret, we will drink to the revolution that will again make Old Mexico the proud country of my fathers. And I, whom you know as Kirk Bannion will be President. I—Esteban Romero—will rule my people."

He jerked the cupboard door open, began to rummage in the shelves.

Jane's glance went to the bedroom. Something stirred there, beyond the partly-open door. Her eyes widened. There was a shadow there, moving across the sunlight on the floor.

Bannion, or Romero, turned to her, a bottle in his hand.

"This is my day," he laughed as he put the bottle on the table.

"Your last day, Bannion, or whatever you call

yourself," said a cold voice. "I heard you, Bannion. I heard you say you killed my father—"

An animal cry burst from Bannion's lips. With the speed of a striking snake he reached for his gun.

The gun in the hand of the tall man framed in the bedroom door sent out leaping spurts of flame. The room rocked to the crash of those three quickly-flung shots from Breck's gun.

Bannion staggered, his half-drawn weapon slipped from limp fingers, and suddenly he crumpled to the floor.

Jane was on her feet, and staring at the cold-eyed man standing there in the doorway, smoking gun in lowered hand.

"Breck!" she cried. "Oh, Breck—" She swayed toward him.

The harsh, implacable lines smoothed out of his face, and suddenly he was smiling.

"You gave us a darn good scare, Jane," was all he said.

Chapter Twenty

The Secret of the Horseshoe

The terrors of the dawn had vanished like smoke in the wind with the coming of Breck and his riders. The harsh desert landscape took on a new beauty for Jane as she gazed at the sawtooth ridge of the Cactus Hills, a wild and violent beauty, perhaps, but a beauty that would no more bring fear to her heart. She knew that she always would love this desert land of the purple sage and bristling cactus, the rolling sand dunes and fantastic painted hills. It was the home of the man she loved.

The thought warmed Jane's heart as the morning sun warmed her body, sent a new zeal for life glowing through her.

Those three sullen-faced men roped to their horses did not seem real to her. They were puppets in a weird and grim drama that she had been watching. There had been a girl in the play who looked like Jane Tallant, but her hero-lover had rescued her and borne her away to Happy-land. The giant red-bearded man on the black horse was Fish Tay, and his two fellow-prisoners were the men who had come with the archdemon of the play, Kirk Bannion, to Mexican Wells.

She heard Breck's voice.

"I hate to do it, Fish Tay, but I'm turning you and your friends over to the sheriff. I'd rather leave you dangling from one of these trees."

"You can't put me in Clem Sorrel's jail," blustered the Box T man. "I'm a respectable rancher . . . I got plenty friends who'll soon have me out of jail."

Johnny Wing snorted.

"I shore don't like his talk, boss. I'm votin' we string these skunks to a tree right now. A rope round their necks is good medicine for their kind."

"I'm votin' with Johnny!" vociferated Dusty Rodes. "Let's swing 'em, boss!"

"It's three to one, boss," chimed in Smoky Peters. "You're out-voted. These fellers will look good to me—dancin' on air."

The three prisoners wilted visibly under the fierce chorus demanding immediate execution.

"Lynchin' is ag'in the law," one of the prisoners muttered. "I'd ruther go to jail—"

"You'd have been full of lead now, only for the boss wantin' to get the drop on Bannion," sneered Dusty. "He told us to get you fellers without any gunplay."

They wrangled on, and Jane, listening from the boulder by the springs, saw the picture—

Breck and his men, crawling with Indian stealth through the mesquite, the silent capture of the unsuspecting men waiting for their satanic leader to finish his sinister work in the cabin. She repressed a shudder.

"I know how you feel, boys," she heard Breck's quiet-voiced decision. "We'll take them to jail and leave them to the Law's hangman."

"Bart Cordy'll have somethin' to say about this bus'ness," muttered Fish Tay.

Dusty Rodes laughed unpleasantly.

"I reckon not, mister," he jeered. "We was bringin' Bart along with us last night. Only trouble is he figgered to make a bolt an' I had to do some quick shootin'—"

"That's right, Fish," grinned Johnny Wing. "You'll see Bart lyin' down the trail a mile or two back."

The red-bearded man cursed them. Dusty's hand went to gun-butt.

"Shut yore mouth," he warned fiercely.

"Take them away, boys," ordered Breck briefly. He addressed Smoky and Dusty. "I want Johnny to ride to the Painted Canyon with Miss Tallant and me."

There was an exclamation from Jane.

"Breck! Those horsemen!" Her voice was startled. "Oh, Breck—they're riding over here—to the Wells!" She sprang to her feet, sudden fear in her eyes.

Silently the others stared at the dun streamers of dust lifting above the arroyo bank. The three prisoners visibly brightened.

"Doggone!" suddenly exclaimed the lynx-eyed Johnny Wing. "It's the sheriff!"

"An' Fred Kelly's Bar K outfit!" exulted Smoky Peters.

Sullen despair wiped the brightening looks from the prisoners' faces. Johnny grinned at them.

"No help for you fellers in *that* outfit," he chuckled.

The cavalcade roared down the winding trail and across the sandy bed of the arroyo to the little oasis of Mexican Wells. In the lead rode tall old Clem Sorrel, and behind him, side by side, galloped a thin little old man and a girl.

Breck felt Jane's hand tighten over his.

"Val Stamper!" The girl's voice was incredulous. "It's Val Stamper—and Della!"

In stunned silence they watched until the riders drew rein. There was a scream from Della. She flung herself from the saddle and ran with outstretched arms to Jane.

"Jane! Oh, Jane! I've nearly died! Thank God, you're safe!"

They held tight to each other, laughing and crying.

Val Stamper dismounted stiffly from his saddle and stood staring at Fish Tay. Slowly he turned and eyed up at the sheriff.

"Do your duty, Clem," he said in his high, raspy voice.

"Looks like Breck has beat me to it," chuckled the old law-officer. He eyed the Circle B man with mock severity. "Was yuh aimin' to decorate yore trees with these jaspers, Breck?"

The latter shook his head, grinned. "They're your meat, Clem. Thought you'd like to make use of that jail you run in Calico."

"Saw Bart Cordy layin' back there on the trail," grumbled the sheriff. "I was fixin' to put that feller where he belonged."

"Do your duty, Clem," repeated Val Stamper impatiently.

"Shore, Val . . . shore I'll do my duty," smiled the sheriff. He pushed his horse close to the prisoners. "Fisher Tay,"—his usually mild voice was suddenly steel hard—"I arrest yuh for the murder of Tom Stamper—"

The red-bearded giant paled. "It's a lie!" he shouted. He jerked his chin in Breck's direction. "He's the feller that killed Tom Stamper."

"You're a liar and a murderer," interrupted Val Stamper fiercely. "Al Roan told me the whole story—how Tom caught you red-handed brand-blotting Horseshoe cows, and how you killed him and pinned the crime on Breck Allen."

Sheriff Sorrel looked at his possemen.

"Take him away, Fred," he said to the Bar K

man. "Turn him an' the other two *hombres* over to Andy Hogan at the jail."

In a moment the possemen were riding away with their prisoners. Jane looked wonderingly at Della's father.

"He—he said you were dead, Mr. Stamper," she faltered. "Kirk Bannion said he had killed you—"

The banker's thin, tired face softened as he gazed at her.

"I've been an old fool, my dear. . . . It is a wonder that I am not dead. Kirk Bannion left orders with Al Roan to kill me." He turned to Breck, held out his hand. "My boy, I'm sorry for all these years of injustice—"

"Forget it," was Breck's brief answer. There was a look in the old man's face that told him some terrible ordeal had chastened him. A kindliness had replaced the avaricious gleam in the eyes, the fierce desire for domination no longer burned in their sunken depths.

Breck gripped the proffered hand with ready forgiveness and all good will.

"I think I'll sit down and rest for a bit," Val Stamper said simply. "My old bones don't seem to take to the saddle like they used to when I was younger. Clem, you tell 'em what happened—" He turned toward a log on the bank of the little stream, eyed back at Jane. "So Kirk Bannion told you I was dead, eh?" He cackled mirth-lessly. "And where is Mister Bannion, young lady?"

Breck answered for her, gestured at the cabin. "In there, Mr. Stamper—"

The old man nodded. "I understand," he commented grimly. "Well, the Devil knows what to do with his own—"

Sheriff Sorrel drew Breck and Jane aside. He had ridden with his posse for the Circle B upon hearing that Fish Tay had been seen near the home ranch, and learning that Breck had left for Calico in search of Jane, had proceeded with his men to the Horseshoe Ranch on the chance the girl had been taken there by Fish Tay. The place was deserted, save for the cook, who had led them to a dugout where Val Stamper had been held prisoner for all the days he had been missing. Bannion had been to see him in a last effort to force him to tell what he knew about the lost mine. Enraged by the banker's claim that he could not tell him anything about the lost lode, Bannion had left, leaving instructions with Al Roan to murder him. The foreman had evidently been unable to bring himself to commit the crime and had ridden away on the raid that resulted in his own death.

"Val was sure that we would find Jane at Mexican Wells," Clem Sorrel told them. "We came on the jump, stoppin' at the Circle B for fresh broncs and to tell Della her father was alive." He chuckled. "Della figgered she would come along with us . . . said it was her fault that Jane got picked up by Fish Tay. Said if she hadn't been at the ranch, her Johnny Wing wouldn't have let you get away like he did."

Breck told the sheriff of Bannion's statement that he had killed old Breck Allen.

Clem Sorrel nodded grimly.

"We've seen the end of lawlessness in this county," he asserted. "You've done a good job, son."

"We're riding up to Painted Canyon," Breck said. "I've an idea about this lost lode."

"Go ahead, son," smiled the old sheriff. "I ain't interested in mines. I'd rather grow a good rose than mine for gold." He went off soberly for a look at the dead outlaw in the cabin.

Val Stamper shook his head when they told him of the proposed visit to Painted Canyon.

"I'm done with looking for gold," he declared frankly. "I've been a crazy man for years, and now I'm sane again. I'll retire to the ranch," he told them wearily. His shrewd old eyes were watching Della and Johnny Wing wistfully. "I'll need a new foreman," he added. "A clean young man like that boy yonder." Val Stamper smiled for the first time that morning, a fond, paternal smile. "It will be up to Della—if Johnny Wing makes the Horseshoe Ranch his home."

Jane laughed softly. "I think," she reassured

him, "that Della and Johnny have already quite made up their minds about the matter, Mr. Stamper."

They rode away alone, up the rugged slopes of the Cactus Hills, leaving Dusty Rodes and Smoky Peters to help the sheriff with certain grim details at the log cabin.

Breck said thoughtfully, "I'll retire old Jim Hawker after fall roundup. He's earned a rest—after forty years with Circle B cattle."

"Jim is one of the best," declared Jane. "Jim and Clem Sorrel—a pair of real old longhorns. I love them both!"

"Dusty would make me a good foreman," mused Breck.

"You won't get him," laughed the girl. "I've an idea that Dusty Rodes is slated for marriage and a cattle ranch of his own—partners with his wife."

"You mean—Letty Gorman?" Breck chuckled. "Well, when they fall—they fall hard. That poor girl deserves a good husband—like Dusty." He laughed loudly, slapped a hard thigh. "Looks like Smoky Peters is due for Jim's place on the Circle B Ranch." He smiled down at her contented face. "Looks like happiness and prosperity will fill the Calico country to over-flowing."

Silence held them as they rode between the high cliffs that guarded the entrance to the

Painted Canyon. Jane pressed her horse close to Breck, assailed by memories of an afternoon when Death had roared down upon her through those grim portals.

"It's beautiful—and dreadful," she said, eyeing the towering painted walls. "The Devil's brush must have painted these cliffs."

There was no trail; the ascent was slow, the horses picking their way between great tumbled boulders.

Jane's face was sober.

"Clem, and Mr. Stamper, think we are looking for a gold mine," she said. "You and I—know differently, Breck—"

He nodded, gaze fixed intently on a huge mass of fallen cliff at the mouth of a narrow gorge that angled into the main canyon.

"I'd always feel happier—to know what happened," Jane added wistfully.

Breck reined his horse and gestured at the rock slide that blocked the entrance to the gorge.

"The Horseshoe Canyon." There was a hint of excitement in his voice. "See, Jane . . . that great mass of rock and earth was once the arch at the mouth of the ravine. You can still make out the outlines . . . the resemblance to the old prospector's map—"

Jane looked at the boulder-choked chasm for a long time. Her face was pale.

"What—what happened?" she finally asked in a low voice.

"An earthquake, perhaps, or natural erosion—a cloudburst," was Breck's guess. And he added gently, "I think we know, now, what happened seven years ago."

The girl's eyes filled. She was silent; and then she said quietly, "We will let him rest there, Breck. The wilderness always called to him—"

Breck had no words. Jane knew that he understood. The lost lode, its waiting riches, seemed insignificant at that moment. They had found something more wonderful than a gold mine . . . no need to hurry about the gold . . . and in the meantime—

Soberly they turned their horses to the sunlight beyond the painted cliffs.

It was *life*—beckoning to them.

Center Point Large Print
600 Brooks Road / PO Box 1
Thorndike, ME 04986-0001 USA

(207) 568-3717

US & Canada:
1 800 929-9108
www.centerpointlargeprint.com

JG